813   Vance, Joel M
        Grandma and the buck deer.

DATE DUE

NE 15 '87	JA 17 '00	
JY 7 '87	SE 06 '00	
AG 19 '87	JA 27 '04	
SE 19 '87	AG 24 04	
OC 7 '87	0 01 15	
OC 28 '87	9-8-22	
July 27	9-28-23	
DE 27 '88		
JA 28 '91		
JAN 20 '94		
AUG 20 98		
OCT 1 9 '95		

DEMCO

GRANDMA AND THE BUCK DEER

GRANDMA

AND THE BUCK DEER

and Other Tales of Youthful Disaster

Joel M. Vance

WINCHESTER PRESS
TULSA, OKLAHOMA

Winchester Press
1421 South Sheridan Road/P.O. Box 1260
Tulsa, Oklahoma 74101

A TALISMAN/WINCHESTER BOOK

Designed by Phil Jaget.

Printed in the United States of America

1 2 3 4 5 84 83 82 81 80

Library of Congress Cataloging in Publication Data

Vance, Joel.
    Grandma and the buck deer, and other tales of youthful disaster.

    1. Sports stories. I. Title.
PZ4.V2214Gr [PS3572.A4235]   813'.54.   80-18537
ISBN 0-87691-322-2

Dedicated to my wife,
Marty—my lantern in the window
at the end of a long, cold day

CONTENTS

ACKNOWLEDGEMENTS

Thanks is due these publications for permission to reprint the following stories which appeared in their original form in those publications:

Field and Stream magazine—"Fishing with Father" (June 1968), "Grandma and the Buck Deer" (June 1969), "We Didn't Do Nothing, Mom" (March 1970), "My Uncle Al's Good Deed" (November 1970); *Weight Watchers' Magazine*—"A Summer Romance" (August 1970), "A Little Game of Snooker" (August 1971); *Yankee* magazine—"The Worst Whipping" (May 1970), "The Day the Durango Kid Got Whipped by a Little Girl" (Entitled: "Go Fly a Monkey") (August 1972); the *Christian Home*—"The School Play" (October 1969—Copyright © 1969 by Graded Press); and the *Kansas City Star Magazine*—"Sweet Smell of Victory," "Downhill All the Way," "Bear With Me," "The Day We Stunk Up The Governor," and "My Father's Million Dollar Garden."

Having spent nearly two days trying to figure out the difference between a preface, foreword, and/or introduction, I was about ready to let this book stand (or, God forbid, topple like a pole-axed shoat) on its own merits.

Grammarians I know insist there is a difference; my grubby old Webster's uses the same words to define each, a sort of grammatical cross-pollination (i.e.: "Foreword, an introductory remark, preface . . .").

So, not knowing what to call these few paragraphs, I almost said the hell with it but decided I needed to explain where some of the characters came from.

Perhaps they should call these mercifully few words the "Author's Advertisement," for it is here that the author is supposed to reveal what angels spoke through him onto the following pages, or else some dignitary (if the author or editor can run one down and threaten him enough) tells you what a real treat is in store for you and how the author can walk on water if he wants to, even if no one ever has seen him do it.

The first written of these stories, "Fishing with Father," was set down in one evening shortly after my father died. His legacy included rare treasures—memories of icy duck blinds, of squirrel hunts together in gumbo-bottom timber, of a bird dog who had trouble finding his food dish, much less quail. "Fishing with Father" is what might have happened.

I owe thanks to the countless girls who sat two rows over and four seats up and for whom I mooned and pined . . . who might have been Margie or Jeannie or Janie or Melody. And other thanks go to various cousins who were, in part or parcel, Hal and Frank.

Uncle Al? Anyone who hunts or fishes knows an Uncle Al. He's the quintessential grubby old river rat. I keep hoping if I live long enough, I'll turn into him.

LET'S GO SEE THE BEARS

My father wanted to get an early start for Birch Lake on Saturday, so we spent all Friday night packing the old Ford. It squatted low in the rear, like a bootlegger's car, but instead of a couple hundred eager horses under the hood all it had was a balky old eight-cylinder junkheap that hammered like a woodpecker. We were moving to the little northwest Wisconsin town where my mother was born. Already the moving van had swallowed up our furniture, which somehow looked impossibly old (not antique, just old) and threadbare and had vanished around the corner.

My father, the former salesman, pointed the peeling nose of the Ford northward. When a family takes a long trip in the smouldering depths of summer, the only thing that keeps it from becoming a savage pack of snarling animals is a fragile veneer of civilized behavior. The bloodthirsty savage is very near the skin of the tight-jawed July motorist. If the trip is long enough, that veneer shatters like Waterford crystal attacked with an eight-pound splitting maul.

We had been driving for two hundred years, give or take a decade, and my father was snarling, my mother was sighing, and I was whining.

"I have to go," I whined.

My mother sighed.

My father snarled. "For crying out loud, why didn't you go when I got gas!"

"I didn't have to then," I said, though I knew he really wasn't asking a question. Shimmers of heat jittered off the pavement and the wind tumbled into the car, hot and unruly. I was hot and sweaty and bored and half carsick and couldn't find a Q in the billboard alphabet game and I had to go to the bathroom and I'd had to leave all my friends and had to go to a new school and it was all my parents' fault.

Stacked up against everything else that happened, the flat tire was a happy event. A blowout, only 30 miles from home. While my father changed the tire and got his new chinos that made him look like Van Johnson greasy from the jack when he dropped it on his foot, a passing car kicked up a pebble that hit him on the ear. That made him dance like an Indian trying to drum up a thunderstorm. He said a couple of things he would have turned my back end red for saying.

A few miles farther on, our old suitcase on the car's luggage rack herniated and clothing exploded merrily through the rupture and fluttered down the highway behind us. The temperature was 97° as my father trotted down the right-of-way, rescuing briefs and brassieres from the path of onrushing automobiles. Heat waves shimmered around his grease-stained legs. He was sweating profusely and clenching his jaws when he dumped everything into the front seat and pulled back on the highway.

"I'm hot," I whined. "Why do we have to stop all the time?"

My father's neck, already pink from the sun, turned a rich burgundy and he growled, just like my old dog when the trash man came. My mother sighed. "I wish we were home," I muttered, continuing to show a persistent inability to keep my mouth shut. My father's knuckles were white on the wheel. The grinding sound either was the transmission about to go out——or his teeth.

Bored, hot, and restless, I picked up my father's rod and reel with which he hoped to catch huge pike and bass if we ever got to

Birch Lake. His tackle box was on the floor. I unsnapped the lid and peered inside at the nest of old fish-gnawed plugs. Veterans all, they lay weary and battle-scarred in their trays. I selected a huge Pikie Minnow, veteran of many a skirmish with sinewy members of the *Esox* clan. *Wonder if it will wiggle in the wind like it does in the water?* I thought. I hooked it on the snap swivel. My parents were paying no attention to me, so I cautiously eased the rod out the window. The wind caught the bill on the front of the plug and stripped off some line before I could stop it.

The whir of the reel caught my father's attention and he looked in the rear-view mirror to see what I was doing.

"Watch out for that car!" my mother screamed as the car ahead suddenly stopped and we didn't. My father stomped the brake and the tires howled. We all bounced forward and the rod flew out of my hand and through the window onto the highway.

We slowed to a stop and sat shaking at the narrow escape. Then my father got out and went back for his rod and reel. There wasn't much left of it. He looked at it for a long moment, then hurled it against a tree. He stalked back to the car, gave me a murderous look, hauled me out of the back seat, and whaled me until I howled.

We got back in the car and I thought about what a tough deal it was to have a father who hated me.

"I bet President Roosevelt's father didn't hate him," I muttered. But not loud enough to be heard.

We continued. Idly, I noticed a sign: "See The Live Bears! 2½ Miles!" Big deal. My father probably would feed me to them.

"See the Vicious Bears! 1½ Miles! Gas! Food! Souvenirs!" All I needed was a bathroom. And a new father if I could swing it.

"Live, Terrible Bears! One Mile!" Damned if I'd ask if we could stop. I was never going to ask anything of that man again.

My father swung the car into a crunching, pitted gravel driveway. A sagging sign said "Restrooms" and I moaned quietly.

"Let's get something to drink," my father said to my mother. "*You* go to the bathroom." As if I were arguing about it.

After I finished, I went into the coffee shop through a screen door so dirty the mesh was clogged to a solid shield. The decor seemed to be Early American Flies. The proprietor was a smudged Neanderthal with a two-day beard and the charm of a roadhouse toilet. "Whatcha gonna have here, Mac?" he growled at my father. "I ain't got all day."

I sat down and promptly knocked over my father's water glass. The water cascaded into his lap. He roared up. "Out! Get out of here!" He brushed ineffectually at the water which had soaked through his grease-stained pants.

Happy Days On The Home Front! The Cro-Magnon smirked at my predicament. I stumpled toward the door, wishing I were in a large, dark closet, hugging a big, friendly dog.

The bright sunlight made me blink. The two bears which formed the rather dubious main attraction of the place were in a massive cage of dirty concrete and rattly steel bars. One bear paced endlessly, brow furrowed with persistent rage, seeking a way out. The other bear, timid and resigned, hunkered in a corner, blankly examining one paw.

A boy about my age with a face like a shrewd opossum stood by the cage. Possumface braced his hands on his hips and looked at the bears with disgust.

"Stupid dumb bear!" he shouted at the pacing animal. "You can't get out. Don't you know that?" The pacing bear looked sourly at us. The other bear continued to look at his paw as if he had never seen it before. It was something to do, I guess.

"Stupid dumb bears!" Possumface said to me. He picked up a piece of gravel and threw it at the mean-looking, pacing bear.

The animal coughed menacingly and pawed at the bars which rattled alarmingly in deteriorating sockets. "Hey!" I exclaimed. "Don't do that!"

"Yeah?" Possumface challenged, "and who are you——their owner or somethin'?"

"You're gonna make that bear mad."

"You can't make a dumb bear mad," Possumface sneered. "He's mad all the time anyway." Possumface was obviously apprenticed to the Wolf Man. "Hey, kid, watch this," he said, a glint of pure sadism gleaming in his piggy little eyes. He popped the bear on the ear with another rock. That earned us a fierce growl and an expression of pure ursine hatred. The shy bear, meanwhile, looked as if it might burst into tears.

"Everett! Everett!" cried a voice as cutting as a buzzsaw. Possumface glanced toward the sleazy cafe, then back at the cage.

"Look!" he cried. "There ain't nuthing keepin' the door shut but a pin." It was true. The hasp was fastened by a linchpin attached to a small chain.

"Everett!" the distant woman shrieked.

"That's my dumb ol' ma," Possumface said.

"Everett!" she keened, spying him. "Leave those dirty old bears alone and come on. We got to go."

Everett cast a last look at the bears. He would miss torturing them, but perhaps his parents would buy him a gerbil he could set on fire.

Inspiration dawned in his buckshot eyes and, before I could do or say anything, he jerked the linchpin from the door, flung it far into the bushes, and fled toward his parents' car which then burst from the parking lot amid a spray of gravel.

Find the pin and put it back! Put the pin back! my mind cried, but my horrified body wouldn't move. It just stood there numbly.

The pacing bear reached the door and, from long habit, tapped it as he turned and started the other way. Only this time the door sagged open with a rusty screech.

The bear had gone one long stride toward the other end before it registered on him that the long-hoped-for miracle had come to pass——the door was open. The bear actually did a double take, like a hirsute Lou Costello.

Quick as a 400-pound weasel, it whirled and battered the door the rest of the way open. We stood there looking at each other. Between me and 400 pounds of bear lay only a dozen feet of very insubstantial air.

The bear paused at the door of its cage, conditioning keeping it inside. But only briefly. It stepped cautiously to the ground, as if testing it for firmness, and swung its massive head, trying to take in all the sights and smells and sounds of freedom with one sweeping gesture.

Then it looked at me and its expression changed from one of wonder and delight to one of definitely threatening interest. Its little eyes (strangely reminiscent of Possumface's) narrowed speculatively, as if it were testing me visually for crunchiness.

My yell of terror, I'm sure, could have been heard clearly one hundred miles away. It even stopped the bear which looked at me in astonishment. My feet wouldn't move. The bear muttered "Woof!" which I didn't interpret as "Hello, how are you?" He reared to full height and curled his lip. It was not a smile. I don't think it could tell the difference between me and Possumface. Somewhere in its little brain, a circuit closed and I became the kid who had hit him on his ear with a rock. The bear growled, a funnel cloud of sound that towered over me with green menace.

It was at that grim moment that my father appeared in the doorway of the shoddy restaurant, having been alarmed by my yell. He said later he didn't remember one thing from the moment he saw me and the bear facing each other like mismatched wrestlers until it was all over.

As the bear paused, possibly choosing a spot for the first bite, my father crashed through the flimsy screen door, cleared the parking lot in about three soaring leaps, and burst past me.

Using the impetus generated by his 30-yard sprint and 170-pound weight, he launched a running roundhouse punch to the bear's nose which was right on target. There was a meaty smack and the bear grunted and shook its head dazedly, then slumped over backward, knocked out colder than Yak sherbet. It was a hell of a punch.

My father never paused. He bounced off the bear, whirled in mid-air, scooped me up, and dashed back to the restaurant. He began to slow down by the time we got to the steps, his adrenal cascade stoppered to a trickle. He looked back. The bear was peacefully sleeping. My father put me down carefully, breathing hard, his eyes wild.

He sat down on the restaurant steps and put his head down. He was trembling. The bear came to, rolled over, and staggered back into the cage. It seemed to be relieved to be home again.

The restaurant proprietor, gnawing his seedy cigar and thinking terrible thoughts of catastrophic lawsuits, trotted apprehensively across the parking lot and locked the cage door.

My mind began to thaw and I looked at my white-faced father. The thought came to me suddenly and with startling impact: *How many kids have a father who knocked out a bear for them!*

I burst into tears and grabbed him and hugged him as hard as I could.

He put his arm around me and said, "Careful, Bobby. I think I broke my hand."

It was a hell of a punch. A hell of a punch . . .

FISHING WITH FATHER

When I was nine, my father took me fishing for the first time——and very nearly the last. He also almost broke my heart.

My father had a lot of people to go fishing with without having to waste his time with a lath-shaped kid with jug ears whose main claim to fame up to that point had been that he had 10 more stitches taken than anyone in the fourth grade.

My father would vanish on Birch Lake before I got up in the morning and only rarely would he return before I went to bed at night. If I did see him, he'd be carrying an imposing stringer of walleyes, pike, bass, and lake perch. He and his friends would sit around the kitchen table at my grandmother's after they had cleaned the fish in the back yard, by the light of a lantern, and they'd relive the day's adventures.

I wanted to go fishing with my father so badly I could taste it, but I was entirely too timid to ask him, especially after I'd broken his favorite rod and reel when we were moving to Birch Lake. Fishing with me never entered his mind. I suspected I didn't, either. But then I never gave him much positive reason to notice me, either. I was skinny as a reinforcing rod and looked quite a lot like a CARE poster child. I had a terrible talent for creating chaos where order had existed. My father never came right out and said it——he was far too decent for that——but I believe he was convinced he'd fathered a dolt.

If I had managed to stay awake until the fishermen came in, docking their flaking old wooden boat with the enormous outboard motor riding its transom like a stripped-down washing machine, I'd watch them trudge up the hill to the house, weary but boisterous. Usually I could keep my eyes open no longer and I'd go to bed on a feather mattress which engulfed me like warm water. The sheets always seemed starchy clean; they smelled of lye soap and rustled like autumn leaves.

The fishing trip with my father started early in the spring, before all the snow had left the city park where the band played, out of tune, on the Fourth of July, the annual charity picnic of the Birch Lake United Civic Clubs and Good Works Society and other functions. The drunker the band got, the better they sounded. Sober, they'd drive everyone else to drink.

I found my father looking speculatively at me one Saturday morning at breakfast. "How would you like to go fishing with me this summer, Bobby?" he asked finally.

Stunned, I tried to swallow an enormous mouthful of Grape Nuts, choked, coughed, and spewed them all over his shirt. When I had wiped my chin and streaming eyes, I croaked, "Oh, gosh! I'm sorry, Dad! Honest! Do you really mean it? Can we go fishing? I mean, really?"

He was occupied with brushing Grape Nuts from his bosom and his face was set and brick red. My father was not noted for his patience and I was certain I'd jinxed the fishing trip. But with a visible effort, he fought down his rage, took a deep breath, and managed to smile at me. "If you can learn to cast well enough, I'll take you out with me," he said. "But you can't catch a fish if you can't cast a lure. We'll go over to the park this morning and start learning."

And we did. We took the old red Ford and drove over to the park where the hardiest squirrels loped along the ground looking for food (and for each other, it being the time to make little squirrels). A few rifts of dirty snow remained in the shadowy spots. But the air was warm where the sun shone.

My father had his fishing rod——a stiff steel shaft five feet long with the action of a fly swatter. His casting reel was equipped with a heavy silk line which was difficult even for a good fisherman to cast.

The instruction began: "Now, you hold the rod up like this," he said, demonstrating the classic casting form. "Use your wrist and forearm," he said, "just like you're flipping mud balls off a stick." Which made little sense since I'd never in my life flipped mud balls off a stick.

He handed me the rod. "Hold your thumb on the reel until the rod is pointed about up here." He moved my arm to the proper angle. "Then release the thumb, but not entirely or you'll backlash." It was every bit as clear as one of his mudballs.

He stepped back, smiling paternally. With sinking heart, for I knew my father expected instant perfection, I brought the rod back. My thumb slipped and the plug fell on the ground behind me.

My face flushed. "I must have let my thumb up," I said. My father nodded. I reeled the plug in and tried again. This time I clamped my thumb tightly down all through the cast until the plug and the rod rebounded off the ground in front of me.

"If you can just arrange to split the difference," my father said with a smile that looked as if it had been assembled with a torque wrench, "you'll be all right."

Amazingly enough, my third try was perfect, the plug traveling in a graceful arc some 30 feet. There was no sign of backlash. The line billowed sumptuously and the plug settled to earth like a fairy landing. I felt a great swelling of joy and my father pounded me on the back. "See!" he exclaimed. "See how easy it is! That was beautiful!" We grinned at each other. It *was* beautiful. It also was the high point of the lesson.

I reeled the plug in, awestruck by my talent. I got set again, cast——and made an inevitable beginner's mistake. I tried for distance, using main strength. The plug shot out about 10 feet before the whizzing reel threw a loop. The plug stopped sharply in mid-air. The rod tip bowed, then straightened, flipping the heavy plug back at me. I ducked and the plug whistled past my ear like a howitzer shell. It hit my father on the side of the head and he yowled, stumbled backward, and fell over a stump into a thorny barberry, planted by the local D.A.R.

I did the only thing possible under the circumstances. I started to cry. Through tears, I watched my father pick himself painfully out of the bush. There was a red mark on the side of his forehead and he rubbed the spot gingerly. He walked around me in a wide arc, not looking at me, occasionally kicking viciously at the leaves. His hands were clenched tightly in fists. Finally he strode over to me.

"I think that's enough for today, Bobby," he said in a high, tight tenor, about a full octave above his normal pitch. "Let's go home, shall we?"

We practiced fitfully a couple more times as the weather warmed, but I noticed each time my father kept a considerable distance from me when I was casting. And each time he was a bit more impatient with my incompetence. Finally, he gave up and told me to practice on my own, which I did until I was fairly proficient at putting the practice plug in or at least near an old inner tube.

I spent one afternoon in the back yard trying to ignore the jibes of my cousin Hal. "Hey, whatcha doin'? Catchin' whales in the dandelions?" He rolled around on the lawn, roaring at his jokes. I handed him a suggestion that would have earned me a whipping if my parents had heard it, then made a perfect cast which ticked the side of the inner tube and slipped inside it. I could almost feel the smashing strike of a big fish.

When my father came home from work that evening, I dragged him to the back yard to watch me.

But even as I picked up the rod, apprehension nattered at my coordination and I knew with dread certainty that I would make a mistake. I knew my father expected me to make a mistake, so of course I did. I threw an enormous backlash.

"I'll have it undone in a second," I babbled. "Just give me a second. I was doing real good this afternoon. Honest I was." I picked at the snarl, but got only long loops that led nowhere.

"Here, let me have it," my father ordered after several minutes. He carried the rod in the house and sat down with the evening paper. He finished untangling the backlash after I had gone to bed. I found the reel restored to neat order the next afternoon. Grimly, I headed for the back yard and more practice.

Then, one June morning when the sun rose like a piece of calendar art, I woke to the smell of frying bacon and my grandmother's incomparable biscuits, swelling with rich flakiness in the oven. The pump handle had a frost of condensation on it when I drew a bucket of cold water. A redbird sat in the grape arbor, amid the pink-green swelling buds and young leaves, and bragged piercingly about what a pretty bird he was.

"How about going fishing this morning?" my father asked. I refrained from coating his shirt with ham and eggs, but it was a near thing. "Oh, yeah!" I cried. "Oh, yeah!"

It was the first time I'd been out in the big old wooden boat. I babbled, skipping to keep up with my father. "Will we catch some fish? I mean, do you think we'll do some catching, Dad?" My mouth sounded out of control, even to me.

"We'll never know if we don't try," he said, screwing down the old motor to the transom. The boat hit the wavelets with the finesse of a boar hog headed for the evening slop, but it got us to Magnussen's Point. We trolled with the wind for a while. My father caught a two-pound walleye, but my deep-running plug went untouched.

"I'll row awhile," my father said. "You cast the shoreline for bass." He pulled the boat in near shore, keeping it about 40 feet off the weed beds. This was the moment when I had to demonstrate what I'd learned in the back yard. I reeled in the plug, feeling the rich excitement of the trip draining out of me.

I took a deep breath and tried to relax. I gritted my teeth . . . and threw the red-and-white plug into an alder which folded over the weeds. My second cast snagged a lily pad and the third didn't travel 10 feet, hitting the water like a washtub full of horseshoes. I knew my father was in agony.

"I want to row, Dad. Please let me row," I begged. Anything to end his irritation and my mortification. He sighed and agreed and I took over the middle seat. I let the line run out from the reel, then set the click and propped the rod against the rear seat. I grabbed the oars and leaned into them.

On the first pull, I caught crabs with both oars and splashed a sheet of water across my father. "It's all right," he said, wiping his face and shivering a bit in the stiff breeze. "Feels kind-of cool. But dig in a little deeper, will you?"

I did well for awhile, but then began to tire. I became sloppy again and my father took some more spray. Overcompensating, I dug more deeply and somehow pulled the right oar out of the lock.

It twisted out of my hand and, before I could grab it, had

drifted several feet from the boat. "Oh, for Pete's sake!" my father cried. He ordered me to the back of the boat and took over with the remaining oar, using it like a paddle.

But it soon became grimly apparent that we were not going to overtake the missing paddle which, gripped in the action of wind and wave, was ever widening the gap that separated us.

Suddenly the reel on my rod, forgotten beside me, screamed as line shot off it in a blur. The rod dipped sharply and nearly leaped out of the boat as I grabbed for it. I glimpsed my father's astonished face, then I found the reel and clamped my thumb down on the racing spool. The line burned a groove in my thumb.

I winced in pain and cried, "Ouch!" but kept the thumb pressed down. Far behind us a lean shape writhed out of the water and hung suspended for a moment against the green hills on the far shore. So magically clear was the moment that I could see my red-and-white plug hanging from the corner of the fish's mouth.

"My God!" my father shouted. "Northern! That's the biggest damn northern I ever saw in my life! Don't lose him!" Although the fight had barely begun, he grabbed his gaff, ready for the landing.

The fish splashed back into the water and bore toward the boat. I reeled frantically, barking my knuckles on the reel handle, sobbing with frustration as the fish gained slack line. But when I caught up with him, he was still there——a savage, cold-eyed creature fighting with reasonless rage at the inexplicable force that thwarted him.

Again and again the fish made keen, swift runs. Then he went to the bottom and lay still, a dead weight. I tried lifting him, but couldn't move him at all. "Hold still," my father said. He reached over with the gaff and slapped it sharply against the butt of the rod. The shock traveled through the stiff rod, down the line and into the fish and he moved off slowly. This time when I pumped against him, he yielded reluctantly. It was the first time I'd felt in command.

"You've got him now," my father said. I noticed he was trembling. "Be careful," he pleaded. "Don't lose him now."

The fish lay on its side, nearly exhausted. So was I. Upright, but nearly exhausted. My father wasn't far from nervous exhaustion himself. He held the gaff hook high like a tennis racket. When the fish slid past the boat, my father took a swipe at him, missed, and nearly fell out of the boat. He moaned.

On the next slow pass, my father sank the hook under the

pike's jaw and flipped him into the boat.

With filial loyalty, I must say that my father made very few mistakes in his life. But this was one. The shock of leaving his element and landing in the boat revived the huge fish unbelievably. It gave one mighty lunge which nearly carried it overboard. Instead, it landed in my father's tackle box which, contrary to his own long-standing closed-lid policy, stood starkly open.

Lures flew in all directions, including the one which had caught the fish. For a moment all I could do was rest my arms, suddenly free of the interminable pressure of the big fish. The northern gave another mighty flop which brought it nearly in my lap. The vicious head reared at me, the cold eyes glaring. I thought it was attacking me for catching it and I screamed, "Help! Dad, help!"

My father snatched up the remaining oar and swung fromthe heels. Just as he started his downswing, the fish rolled toward him and lashed its powerful tail across his knees. Unbalanced, he struggled wildly for balance. The oar shot from his grasp and splashed yards away in the lake. My father tripped over the front seat and fell painfully into the space between it and the bow. The boat rocked dangerously.

But that was the mighty fish's final bid for freedom. We all lay dazedly in recumbent positions. But my father and I had a bit more resilience than the pike and recovered our wits more quickly.

My father got a stringer on the fish, then put on a second for insurance. He tied them both securely to the empty oarlock on the port side, then wrestled the huge fish overboard.

The fish lay on its side, gills moving slowly, for a minute or so, then righted itself and lay in the water, held to us by the stringers. For the first time in many minutes he had time to think. My father ruefully surveyed the wrecked, oarless boat.

"I don't know if you've thought about it or not," he said to me. "But we're in a hell of a fix." Strangely, he didn't sound a bit upset about it.

It was nearly dark before we were able to hail a passing boat and get a tow into the town dock. We drew a big crowd of Birch Lakers as soon as the word got out, and I spent the next hour flushing pleasurably, embarrassed but happy, as a stream of fishlookers plied me with questions: "Howja hookim? Where wereya at? How muchee weigh? L'il bitty squirt like you pull in that fish? Heckuva fish, kid!"

Finally they all left and we ate supper. Afterward, my father and I sat back and looked at each other. By some mute agreement, we rose simultaneously and went back outside. We lit the coal oil lantern and hung it on a nail above the rough wooden table on which my pike was laid out.

We stood looking at the huge fish, its skin now dried and dull, its eyes glassy.

And then my father draped his arm around my shoulders—— not the way he would with a child, but the way he did with his fishing buddies. It was a companionable, natural, warm gesture.

I had never known such a happy moment.

THE SCHOOL PLAY

It all started with a note home from Miss Allendale, my fifth-grade teacher, a wispy young woman who always looked on the verge of tears and carried herself with the nervous anxiety of a house wren.

"Here's the word from the birdies to tell you the fifth grade has decided to make up a little assembly to entertain you. All the children want to invite you to the school auditorium on Oct. 14 at 8 p.m."

I read the note on the way home from school and felt like gagging. "Word from the birdies, for Pete's sake!" I exclaimed. Miss Allendale's prose could put a diabetic into a coma. She had spent most of the afternoon studying each of us pensively, a bit apprehensively (though it was hard to tell since she always seemed apprehensive), gnawing a pencil eraser and frowning. Occasionally, when her glance rested on a particular kid, a tiny birdflicker of a smile would wriggle over her mouth and she'd write something down on a pad of paper, then resume her reverie.

We found, in the last hour, that she'd been casting her epic which, contrary to the implication in the note, had been conceived and written by Miss Allendale. It was entitled, "Children of the World," and featured simple songs, dances, and situations from history and legend. She assigned our parts just before school's end.

"Bobby," she told me, handing me a smudged mimeographed script, "you'll be the little Dutch boy who saves Holland by putting his finger in the dike. You're the hero. The whole play revolves around you."

Well, now, that sounded a bit of all right. With the massive confidence of Richard Burton, I said, "Okay, I guess I'll take it then."

My first speech was a soliloquy which wasn't destined for the required reading list in English Lit., but which was, like Miss Allendale, childishly direct: "I'm just a poor little Dutch boy and nobody likes me. Nobody pays any attention to me. If only I could do something to make people notice me. I wish I could be a hero!"

That Miss Allendale sure could write!

After my oration, I was supposed to slump dejectedly beside the dike while a group of children trundled onstage and sang a tender ballad entitled, "The Little Dutch Boy," composed by Miss Allendale (lyrics) and the band director (melody).

"All alone he walked by the Zuider Zee,
Not a friend in the world had he.
He thought he'd never, never be big . . .
All alone like a friendless pig."

I suspected Miss Allendale was stuck for a rhyme on the last line, grasping at lyric straws, because I couldn't see how a lonesome Dutch kid and an unhappy pig jibed. "Water squirts through set behind Dutch boy," the script directed. "The dike has burst!" I was to cry upon seeing the water.

But there was no one to hear me, so I plugged the leak by sticking my finger in it, saving Holland from the angry seas. Pretty neat stuff for a 10-year-old. Since practical time limitations precluded me waiting as long as the original Little Dutch Boy waited for help, the passage of time was explained by a little girl at stage right:

"Many, many hours waited he,
Holding back the raging sea.
Almost exhausted, he waited alone,
Like a hungry dog waiting for a bone."

Miss Allendale was a great one for animal simile. The play

had a happy ending. The fifth grade didn't go in for grim realism. Just as I was near the end of my endurance, finger blue, someone happened along, found me, and sounded the alarm. After that, everyone burst on stage shouting, laughing, and singing about what a hero I was.

I ran all the way home and into the kitchen yelling, "Mom! I'm in a play at school! I'm the hero! I save Holland!"

"Well," she said, rolling a chicken leg in flour, "before you save anything, go up town and get me a loaf of bread."

"Ma! I can't! I gotta practice!"

"Bread, then practice." I could see John Wayne trudging off to town, stepping on his lower lip, to get *his* mom a loaf of bread. Uh-huh.

By the time my father came home, I'd learned my part. I dragged my parents into the front room and forced them to listen to me emote. I gave it everything I had. "That's just fine," my father said, rattling the Birch Lake *Beacon.* "Which one of the Three Pigs did you say you were?"

Rehearsals went well for the first week. I was ready for the big night, but I wasn't too sure about Miss Allendale. She grew increasingly nervous as First Night approached. It was her first production and she had a thriving case of the jitters. When someone forgot his lines, she gulped. When the chorus lost the melody and wandered off in different musical directions like grazing sheep, she blanched. When the Russian dancers fell down, she moaned.

The Russians gave her most of the trouble. Ten youngsters stubbornly refused to learn the steps to a peasant dance, and when they finally did get the steps right they lost their balance and fell down. Several boys threatened mutiny because they had to put their arms around girls. Miss Allendale cajoled, begged, and threatened, but the Russians remained stoically wrong.

Finally the big night came and all over Birch Lake fathers swore as they struggled into unfamiliar suits, mothers hovered, mouths full of pins, and youngsters wiped sweaty palms and tried to quiet galloping hearts.

There was a sense of excitement outside the school when we got there. The night was filled with running, chattering kids. Parents talked in the crisp dark about late-season fishing and early-season hunting. The auditorium was full of the shuffle and clack of seats being lowered and raised. The curtain billowed as someone backstage bumped into it. I went backstage for makeup and last-minute instructions from the harried Miss Allendale.

I found the group of Dutch boys and girls. As if it had been waiting for me to arrive, trouble started. Little Mary Magee, who was to be the narrator of my scene, suddenly said, "I don't feel so very good," and threw up.

She started to cry and two members of the chorus joined her. Miss Allendale came running across the stage, her eyes wide and worried. "What's the matter!" she cried. "What's the matter!"

"Ain't nothin', lady," said the janitor, instantly on the spot with a mop and bucket. "Little kid just pitched her cookies. Happens every time we gotta 'sembly."

When Miss Allendale saw what had happened, she nearly fainted, but pulled herself together and sent someone to find Mary's parents to tell them what had happened. They soon came backstage and led their sobbing daughter toward the exit. That left us without a narrator for the middle of the scene. Miss Allendale made a quick, panicky survey of the survivors and finally drafted a little girl from the chorus. She gave the girl a copy of the narration to study in a quiet corner.

She wiped her brow, cast her eyes briefly skyward, and rushed off to quiet a pair of pigtailed girls who were arguing loudly about the relative size of their roles.

Some of Mary's mal-de-theatrics began to communicate itself to me. A film of cold perspiration broke out on the palms of my hands. Trying to calm myself, I decided to practice my big speech, the final one, and found to my utter horror that I couldn't recall even the first word. I made a frantic grab for my battered script and looked at the speech. Each sentence looked as foreign as Senegalese.

It was curtain time. Oh, horrors! Miss Allendale shushed us and hustled everyone offstage except the first-scene players. The rest of us huddled back in the wings while the curtain rose on a Gypsy scene. Through the side curtains, I saw a dim mass of faces, bathed in the hazy glow from the footlights. The crowd coughed and shuffled its many feet, like some monstrous centipede with catarrh.

I tried to choke down a walnut-sized lump in my throat. The Gypsy dancers whirled and rattled their tambourines. Everything was going well until one little boy let go of his tambourine in the middle of a less-than-graceful pirouette and watched it sail out over the footlights into the audience.

There was a faint tinkle and crash from the darkness as it landed and a louder crash from the stage as a second dancer ran into the first, knocking both of them down. A third dancer fell over the first two and everyone else stopped uncertainly.

Miss Allendale cried in a voice clearly audible at the back of the auditorium, *"Pull the curtain! Pull the curtain!"* There was a rustle of nervous laughter from the audience and Miss Allendale turned an unhealthy ivory color.

The next act, however, was uneventful and both she and I settled down somewhat. The missing speech began to come back to me. It was nearing time for the Dutch act and I thought I'd better have someone put on my makeup. Three harassed mothers had volunteered (much against their better judgment) to paint the faces of the players and they now were fluttering and swabbing frantically to keep up with the rush.

I managed to edge in front of a boy in the line leading to one of the makeup women. "Hey," he exclaimed, grabbing me by the shoulder. "I was here first. Go back to the end of the line." He pushed me and that made me mad.

"Nuts to you," I said. "I gotta get my stuff on."

"Now boys," said the makeup mother between dabs with a powder puff. "Be quiet and don't argue. They'll hear you." She motioned toward the audience with her puff.

The boy paid her no attention and shoved me again. "Get back there or I'll hand you a fat eye!" he hissed.

"You and what army, dummy?" I sneered. He jumped at me and I dodged. The makeup mother stepped back in alarm and raised her hands to quiet us. Her heel came down on the bare foot of a little girl in a Hawaiian costume.

The girl gave a high scream of pain and the woman clawed desperately for her balance. She grabbed the nearest support which happened to be the setting at the side of the stage. The scenery had been designed to withstand normal wear and tear, but not a sudden assault by a full-grown woman.

The setting began to topple, then crashed, carrying the woman with it. The two of them landed in full view of the audience with a thunderclap sound as the flat hit the stage floor. All motion stopped onstage. Several little boys giggled and the little girls blushed under their makeup. The fallen mother was crimson. Again the curtain was hastily pulled in the middle of an act. There was hearty laughter, mostly male, from the audience.

The mother scrambled to her feet and shouted, "If I get my hands on those two little brats, I'LL WRING THEIR NECKS!"

I melted into the crowd, my nerves singing like telephone wires. I caught a glimpse of Miss Allendale, quietly crying, the tears streaming unchecked down her wan cheeks. Two prop men replaced the fallen setting and Miss Allendale weakly signalled for the next act to begin. She had resigned herself to whatever damnation results from artistic catastrophes. She was going through the motions of running her dream production, but her heart wasn't in it. Miss Allendale was a broken woman. Her shoulders hunched in dejection. Her movements were wooden and automatic and her eyes lifeless. Her hair was disarrayed. Could nothing revive her shattered spirits? I felt a great wave of compassion for her. Perhaps the Dutch skit would be such a blinding artistic triumph that all would be saved. I owed it to her for her faith in me. I could do no less than bring the audience to its feet, cheering, shouting "Bravo!" or whatever Birch Lake audiences shouted when they liked something.

Amazingly, the tottering drama righted itself for the next two skits. A number about Mexico, featuring Miss Allendale's vision of the Hat Dance, went off without a hitch and drew a healthy round of relieved applause. The skit just before mine, dealing with Hawaii, was perfect except for a slight limp from one of the hula girls.

The audience was receptive and the performers in the Dutch skit, sensing that conditions were perfect for a socko finish, were cocky and eager to have at it. Everything seemed right for a smash finale. I poised in the wings, waiting for the curtain, exhilaration flooding me. This would be, I felt sure, the beginning of a dramatic career which would eclipse that of Johnny Mack Brown or even the Durango Kid.

The curtain rose.

I strode confidently from the security of the wings to the middle of the intensely lighted stage, alone and composed, the hush of the expectant audience almost palpable.

And suddenly a fantastic thing happened. I realized that hundreds of critical eyes were fixed on my every move. I was sure my fly was open, assuming I even was wearing pants. My soul flooded with incalculable terror. In less time than a lightning flash, my mouth went as dry as Death Valley, my limbs lost their coordination, and my eyes wallowed out of focus. Fright bollixed my motor processes and I probably would have collapsed, except that every joint was as frozen as if I'd gotten a cement transfusion. All I could hear was a great roar, like the sea, and when I tried to lick my lips, they were stuck together so tightly I couldn't force my tongue between them.

Dimly I saw white faces of other children on the other side of the stage, waiting for their cue, but I couldn't break the log jam in my head. I stood rooted in panic for several million years, then very distantly heard a voice saying, "I'm just a poor little Dutch boy . . ."

I heard the phrase over and over again without realizing it was a hissed cue from backstage. Finally the repetition triggered something and I croaked, "I'm just a poor little Dutch boy . . ."

Once the wheels were in motion, I lost a bit of my fright and was able to finish the speech, even though it lacked much depth of feeling. I walked woodenly over to the dike painted on the rear stage flat. There was a tiny trickle of water which I was not, at first, supposed to notice. I didn't. I didn't notice anything.

The chorus came on stage and warbled rather raggedly through the Friendless Pig piece and then crowded offstage like a mob racing for a commuter train. They should have been arrested for leaving the scene of an accident.

Dutifully, I discovered the leak. Or rather, it discovered me. I was sitting directly in front of the hole and someone turned the hose behind the scenery on full force. The water hit me squarely in the back of the neck.

"The dike has burst!" I cried, then shouted, "Turn off that stinkin' water!" I leaped to my feet. The audience roared, throwing me into another web of confusion. Galvanized by the laughter, I jammed my finger into the hole and a piercing wave of pain swept up my arm. I had sprained the finger.

Someone behind the set was cursing softly as he tried to turn off the water. I had poked the hose out of the hole when I stabbed my finger in it and the hose was lashing around behind the scenery. Water seeped under the backdrop.

I sat with my back to the audience, ashamed to face them, and hoped that if death wouldn't strike suddenly and end this, at least that I would faint and not revive until everyone in the audience had grown old and died.

The substitute for the little girl who had gotten sick marched out to the edge of the stage and promptly dropped her script into the orchestra pit. She stood there panic stricken for at least a lifetime, then burst into wails and had to be led off by one of the makeup mothers.

My finger was throbbing and I decided to take it out of the hole for a rest. I didn't think anyone would notice in the general confusion at the other side of the stage. To my horror, I discovered that the finger had swelled and I couldn't budge it, no matter how hard I tugged. "My finger's stuck," I whispered, hoping the man who had been swearing at the hose would hear me. But nothing happened. I glanced at the front of the stage where the little girl was starting to read her speech from a new script. Evidently Miss Allendale had become grimly determined to finish the evening come hell or—— appropriately enough——high water. I began to sweat.

I pulled harder at the swollen finger and felt the entire setting stir slightly. It teetered at the top. I bit my lip and eased off the pressure.

The little girl finished her speech and the chorus came onstage and began to chant, "He's a hero! Look what he's done! He's stopped the water! He's saved Holland!"

I whispered to the nearest kid that I couldn't get my finger out of the dike, but he didn't hear me. Two boys rushed over to me, carrying a bucket and a trowel.

"Get your finger out," one of them hissed. "We're supposed to fix the dike."

"I can't," I told them. "It's stuck."

"Come *on!*" the second kid grated.

"It's stuck!" I repeated a bit louder. I was getting mad.

"You better get your finger out or Miss Allendale will fan you good," the first boy warned.

"I can't!" I almost shouted. "My finger's stuck!"

"*I'll* get it out!" declared the second boy. He clenched his jaws tight and grabbed my arm. I started to shout a warning, but too late. He gave my arm a mighty jerk.

The setting started to topple as my finger came loose. The thing hung in midair for a long time and we all scrambled out of the way. It came down with a crash and a whoosh of air which nearly blew out the front three rows. There were screams and shouted exclamations and, through the hole created by the fallen set, I saw Miss Allendale, her mouth working, her face blotchy.

The stage was a shambles and so was Miss Allendale's show. The next few moments were confused. I found my parents in the crowd of people who had rushed to the stage to collect their threatened youngsters. One Little-League mother even had the gall to corner poor, terrified Miss Allendale and yell at her for quite awhile.

I begged my parents to take me home, cried all the way, went to bed as quickly as I could get my clothes off, and curled into a tight, fetal ball.

Miss Allendale never said a word about what had happened, but I noticed that she never called on me for anything the rest of the time I was in her class. She was married to an army lieutenant at the end of the school year and quit teaching entirely. I never saw her after that.

The day after the assembly, I decided to become a Texas Ranger when I grew up.

THE WORST WHIPPING

I recall my childhood whippings with a great deal of painful precision and a faint afterglow in the seat of my pants. But the time I lost my father's new $55 fishing outfit to a hobo from a passing Hayward, Ladysmith and Great Northern freight train was the worst in duration and intensity.

Yet it was the best whipping I ever earned.

My father bought a Pflueger Supreme reel and a snazzy rod on which to display it. "Now, listen, Bobby," he told me, enunciating carefully. "I want to make it very clear that you are not to touch this rod. Ever. Under any circumstances. Is this clear?" My father once told me I was the only kid he knew who could break Jello.

"What if the house is burning down?" I asked. He looked at me for a long time and I blushed.

The outfit was a beautiful thing, all oiled symmetry and quiet elegance. My old reel sounded like a gravel crusher and sometimes bound so tightly that Charles Atlas would have herniated trying to loosen it.

It was all my parents' fault. They should have known better than to leave me alone for an entire day. Especially me. But they went to Rice Lake for a day of shopping, leaving me to get into trouble all by myself. I mosied around.

My cousin Hal showed up just as I got out my old reel and cast at a back-yard bucket. If there were any doubt I could get into trouble by myself, Hal would dispel that. If trouble was having trouble occurring, Hal inevitably proved a perfect catalyst.

There was a bit of grit somewhere in what my Aunt Helen delicately called the "inwards" of the old reel, but what I called the guts. The first cast brought a sound like Andy Devine singing, and everything froze as tight as a convention of drunks.

"That's the mangiest reel I ever saw," Hal sneered. "You couldn't catch cold with that junkpile."

"Yeah, well maybe so!" I shot back intelligently. Stung by his criticism, I bragged, "But I bet my Dad's new reel is the best you ever saw."

"Another of them dollar ninety-eight pieces of junkyard crud?"

Hal often got to me. He was so . . . so *right* all the time. There's nothing worse than a cousin who's right all the time.

"It's the best rod and reel I ever saw!" I said hotly.

"Bring it out then, if it's such hot stuff."

"I can't. Dad would fan me good."

"You're scared to. You're chicken."

"Am not!"

"Chick, chick, chick!"

"You shut up!" I ran into the house, nearly ripping the screen door off, and grabbed up the beautiful rod and reel. "How do you like that, you big dumb!" I shouted, thrusting it at Hal.

"Whew!" Hal breathed. "That's some outfit!"

We looked at it and, now that I had it outside in the summer sun, it didn't seem like much of a crime. After all, I'd take it back pretty soon and no one would know I'd touched it. I wasn't going to hurt it. One little cast surely wouldn't be harmful. I thumbed the reel and flipped the Bass-Oreno on the end of the line into the bucket with consummate ease. The line flowed off the richly humming spool like butter slipping across a hot frying pan.

"I believe I could cast that old plug down a rathole and never touch the sides," I said.

"Let's go fishing," Hal suggested instantly. "Uncle Al says there's big pike over by the town dock."

"No! I can't do that . . ."

"Aw, who's gonna know? Come on!" The more I thought about hooking a big northern on that dream outfit, the less I considered the consequences of disobeying my father.

We had to cross the railroad tracks, then go through a patch of woods to get to the lake. We heard a train coming, far down the track——its hoarse, lonesome call as melancholy as that of a tundra goose. "Let's sit here till that old train goes by," Hal said, flopping down at the bottom of the rail bed. "We can wave at the engineer. Let me see that good ol' rod and reel."

I hesitated and he insisted, "Come *on*! Don't be chicken." I could see him chanting "chick, chick, chick!" again and reluctantly handed him the outfit. The train hove into view, hacking smoke and noxious fumes and staggering down the tracks like some alcoholic robot.

When the engine went past, we gave the engineer the traditional arm-pumping hurry-up signal. He glared down and loosed a squirt of tobacco juice which narrowly missed us. So much for Norman Rockwell's America. *"I hope you run out of steam!"* Hal screamed after the clattering engine. "Grouchy old goat." He looked down at the fishing outfit in his hands and a sly look flickered on his face, as ominous as a green clam in a bowl of chowder.

"Gimme it back," I said apprehensively.

"Just a minute," Hal said, studying the rocking train.

"Come on," I pleaded anxiously. "Give it here."

"In a minute. Hey, bet a million I can put that plug in the next open boxcar door!" Hal exclaimed suddenly.

"Hey! No!" I shouted frantically.

"There!" Hal cried. "Now!" He cocked his wrist and let fly, leading the open door instinctively, like a duck hunter swinging on a swift teal. The red-and-white plug arced true through the gleaming day, trailing its billowing tail of 20-pound test braided line.

A bleary-eyed hobo stepped into the opening, rubbing his gritty whiskers and blinking. The Bass-Oreno pounced right in the middle of his chest and the ganged treble hooks grabbed him as if the lure were a falcon stooping to a hapless field mouse.

Instinctively, Hal jerked back. The hobo, firmly leashed to

Hal and off balance, cried thinly, "What the hellllllll!" and sailed into the air. He hit the rail bed with a crash, sending gravel and dust into the air.

"Shazam!" breathed Hal, a fan of Captain Marvel.

The hobo stopped rolling and flapping and staggered to his feet. He grabbed the line, looked at the Bass-Oreno dangling from his shirtfront and began to look for what was on the other end of the line. He was an ugly-looking customer, and his villainous looks hadn't been improved by plowing them through the gravel.

He scowled fearsomely. The scowl promised he would use our arms as bludgeons on the rest of us if he caught us. "Cummon!" Hal cried, dropping the rod. "Run for your life!"

We fled through the ragweeds. Some time later, reason returned, bringing with it the awful knowledge that I had left my father's fabulous fishing outfit in the company of a man of probable low repute.

I went home in lock step with abject fright and waited for my parents as one awaits the gibbet. They came home and I followed my father's progress through the house with the quivering ears of a bayed rabbit. "Lake is like glass," he said, ". . . go fishing for a while." Words of doom. "Did you move my fishing stuff?"

Rummaging sounds. "Wonder if Bobby knows . . . Bobby! Bobby! Oh, here you are. Bobby, have you seen my new rod and reel?"

All afternoon I had been trying to think of a good, believable lie——that a tornado had jerked it out the window, that spies had overpowered me and taken it, or (most improbable of all) that I didn't know anything about it.

"I was just going to try it out," I whimpered, near tears.

"Where is it?" he asked, his voice sounding like Uncle Al's old canoe being dragged across a gravel bar.

"A bum took it," I said miserably. I babbled out the tale in a torrent of words, anxious to get rid of the burdensome, sour-tasting confession.

"You did . . . you caught . . . he fell . . . what kind of a . . ." My father paused for a deep, ragged breath, fighting to regain tenuous control over his easily aroused temper. "Now, once again, what happened to my rod? And this time I want the truth. Don't you lie to me!"

"It is the truth," I muttered stubbornly.

"Bobby, come *on!*" he exclaimed. "What happened?"

"That's what really happened," I said sullenly.

"That's the most disgraceful bunch of nonsense I've ever heard!" shouted my father. "You lose my rod and you lie about it!"

He folded me across my bed and jerked my jeans down, a humiliating experience. He began thinking of his beautiful, lost outfit and really leaned into his work. "Now, I want the truth!" he demanded, red-faced.

"It is the truth!" I sobbed. He stormed to the door and slammed it behind him. It wasn't the whipping, though that really hurt. But I had that coming. What really hurt was that he didn't believe me. He taught me always to tell the truth, and when I did, he wouldn't believe it. That was why I cried in my room and wanted to die. Dinner that night was a somber affair.

Then my Uncle Floyd came in. He owned the Birch Lake tavern. He plopped down. My father was taut with anger. My mother was fussed that her oft-errant chick had strayed the coop once again.

"Damndest thing happened a while ago," Uncle Floyd said. "This old bum comes in with a brand-new rod and reel. Must have been worth fifty-sixty dollars. The rod, I mean. The bum I wouldn't give you a nickle for. Tried to swap the stuff for a bottle of booze. Said he needed a drink bad.

"The town marshal was there and started tryin' to find out what's goin' on. Never seen anyone as scraped up as this bum was. Finally claimed some kid jerked him off a train with a big red-and-white plug and that rod and reel. Ain't that the damndest story you ever heard?"

Uncle Floyd looked around expectantly, only to discover everyone was looking at me. I saw the white, shocked face of my father and then I jumped up, turning over my chair, and ran for the door. Blindly I ran into the evening cool. I ran until I was too tired to run any more. Then I sat down and watched an ant trying to take a crumb of food somewhere. The crumb was so enormous that the ant staggered and fell repeatedly.

"Bobby?" It was my father. He sat down beside me and I picked up a pebble and threw it at the ant. Predictably I missed. My father cleared this throat. Then we sat some more and I threw another rock at the ant. I missed again.

"You *did* deserve a whipping for disobeying me," he said.

"You didn't spank me for that," I said. "I told you the truth, but you didn't believe me. That's why you whipped me."

The ant reached his hole and staggered down it while other ants brushed impatiently by him, looking for their own crumbs. I glanced at my father. His eyes were on me, steady and thoughtful.

"Bobby, I'm sorry," he said. "It's all I can say. I'm sorry I didn't have faith in you."

It was at the same time the easiest thing he could have said——and the hardest. Then he hugged me up tight to him, the way he did when I was little and skinned my knee.

That's what made it the best whipping I ever had.

THE DAY THE SPIES
HIT BIRCH LAKE

Elmer Blosser was the town marshal in Birch Lake. They said he was the only town marshal in Wisconsin who never ran in the town drunk because he *was* the town drunk.

The town paid him a salary which would have had to be raised to be called a pittance. Elmer rounded up the rest of his boozing money by doing odd jobs, some odder than others, including plumbing, hauling garbage, and cleaning septic tanks. Birch Lakers tried very hard to stay upwind of him.

Considering his aromatic avocations, it's no wonder he spent most of his money on beer.

He downed vast quantities of it at my Uncle Floyd's tavern and muttered about spies. Elmer was obsessed with the idea that spies not only threatened his beloved United States (How can anyone be a superpatriot whose democratic opportunity has resulted in a career as a septic tank cleaner?), but that Birch Lake was a strategic target on a par with the Pentagon.

And somewhere in his beer-inflamed daydreams, Elmer had the idea that he could gain respectability by capturing spies. With the simple faith of the very stupid, he felt he had the mental and physical tools for dealing with the enemy, lacking only opportunity.

The more alcohol he soaked up, the more positive he became. "Any day now," he'd growl, curling a dirty hamfist around a glass of Bruenig's Lager, "they'll push the button and the whole damn state will go up. Barrrroooom!" He'd turn to the potato farmer nearest him and jab him midways of his Big Smith overalls with a meaty finger. Belching thunderously, he'd rumble, "You think ol' FDR don't know about all them spies? Why the hell do you think there's so many of them? How about that, huh!"

His victims would nod some sort of vague agreement and head quickly for the street.

Hal and Frank and I had little on our minds that bright and blinding August afternoon, except a few rounds with the shooting machine which glittered and gibbered in one corner of Uncle Floyd's bar.

It was one of those machines with a lot of flashing lights, grinding noises, bells and loud explosions. When fed a nickle, it went through its hysterical paces with electronic enthusiasm. There was a gun fastened to it which resembled a .30-caliber water-cooled machine gun. Little Japanese Zeros zipped across a tin sky. We shot beams of light at the planes and, if they were hit, the machine belched and carried on dramatically for several seconds. I was the leading ace of the pre-acne set.

Hal liked to create his own dialogue, lifted mostly from John Wayne war movies, as he played on the machine: "There he goes! Behind you, Hal, behind you! Rat-tat-tat-tat! That'll teach you to say the hell with Babe Ruth, slanteyes! Take that, you dirty rat! Rat-tat-tat-tat!"

While he was bringing down the Imperial Japanese Air Force, I noticed Elmer, ballooning over his bar stool, overflowing the seat like a bride's first attempt at cooking rice. His belt loops, strained to the limit, threatened to snap as he leaned forward to inhale another glass of Bruenig's. His checkered shirt was out at the tail. His gray denim pants were stained. His nickled badge was worn, showing brass highlights.

Elmer wore a huge, ancient pistol at his hip. His cartridge belt was so old the leather was cracked like a July mudflat. The cartridges were corroded. Elmer's Hoover Dam of a belly supported a round, seamed, pitted face that looked like a moonscape. His gravelly voice reverberated through the bar with the insistent clatter of BBs falling on a drumhead.

"Seen where that factory burned down to Mississippi!" He clattered. "Then damn Nazis, I bet. Better not no spies try anything here in Birch Lake. Never know. I seen a guy get off the bus this morning. Looked pretty shifty to me."

"Why don't you go check him out?" his barstool neighbor suggested, hoping Elmer would leave.

Elmer peered suspiciously at the man. "I know my job," he snarled. "You tryin' to tell me my job?"

The farmer made a hasty disclaimer and headed out back. Elmer was a mean drunk (which meant he was mean most of the time). He hated kids. I think he resented our clear eyes.

"You kids! Get away from that there thing!" he shouted, spying us at the gun machine. "Floyd, what you want to let them brats in here for anyway?" Elmer asked. He glared at us and we shuffled out on the seamy old sidewalk and tried to decide what to make of life for the next few hours.

"Old bag of guts!" I exclaimed.

"Nuts to him," Hal said. "You wanta go swimming?"

"Nah," I said——because I was the only one who didn't even know how to dog paddle and it embarrassed me to wade around in the shallows like a girl.

"Well, let's do *something!*" Frank broke in. We glared at him. He deflated. Youngest and therefore lowest in the peck order, he still needed reminding sometimes. Occasionally with a fist.

"You hear Jack Armstrong last night?" Hal asked me.

"Naw——Grandma's tubes are busted and she won't get them fixed."

"Hey!" Hal exclaimed suddenly. "I got an idea." He insisted on secrecy until we got to the town ice house, one of our hideouts. It was in a weed-choked lot behind the lumberyard. Townspeople cut the ice off Birch Lake in the winter and stored it in sawdust for the many townspeople who still cooled food with it.

We slipped through a small hole in the back door of the old wooden building. The air inside was cool. We clambered to the loft and pushed the loading door partly open so we could watch the world pass. Hal pushed his blond, almost white hair back with a tanned hand.

"You know Old Lady Gunnison?" he asked.

I knew her all right, a crotchety witch who screeched at any kid with guts enough to come within 50 feet of her yard. Once she'd caught me trying to pry a slat loose from her fence.

"What are you doing!" she screeched at me, looking like the Wicked Witch of the East, North, South, and West. I gulped. I had needed the slat to hit a big ugly bug which had given me a menacing look, but she scared me so badly I couldn't explain and just stood there looking stupid and afraid.

"You get off my property, you little wretch!" I wasn't sure what a wretch was, but thought it had something to do with throwing up——which was what I was on the verge of doing.

"You get out of here and don't you ever come back!" she hissed. She would have made a great comic-book villain called the Hooded Adder.

"Yeah," I said to Hal. "I know her. So what?"

"You know that old barn out behind her house?"

"Yeah."

"You know what's up in the loft?"

"For cry eye, how would I know. I've never been there."

"I have." Hal smirked.

"Awwww" I scoffed.

"Have too! Know what I found?"

"No."

"Wanna know?"

"No."

"Aw, *crap!*"

"Okay then, what's up there?"

"Ain't gonna tell you."

"Aw, cummon."

"Go climb a stump."

"Cummon, cummon," shouted Frank, forgotten until now, so excited I thought he'd wet his britches.

We glared at him and he shut up.

"Okay," I said, "then what's up there?"

"Not 'til you tell. I ain't gonna let that ol' lady shoot me for something I don't know what it is."

"Huh?" Hal asked, fuddled.

"Tell me first."

"No."

"Cummon."

"No."

"Aw, *crap!*"

We sat, not looking at each other, digging at the wet sawdust. Frank looked from one to the other. "Well, *ain't* you gonna tell him!" he squeaked in exasperation. "If he don't wanta know, I do! *I* wanta!"

"He says he don't wanta know," Hal said sulkily. "If he don't, then the hell with him."

"Well, *I* wanta know! *I* wanta know!" Frank shouted, so frustrated he was on the verge of tears. He growled like a mean dog and kicked the wall and then hopped around the loft moaning. He'd forgotten the toe was out of his sneaker.

"You wanta know?" Hal challenged me directly.

"Big fat deal," I said. "Okay, I wanta know, too!"

We reconnoitered the rear of the Gunnison place. It was about a hundred yards from my Uncle Floyd's tavern and separated from it by a weed-grown old field. Old Lady Gunnison's barn was a rakish old relic, tilted drunkenly to one side, silvered by the years. We skulked through the sunflowers along the fence behind her house. The back windows peered suspiciously at us. We slipped quickly, one by one, into the barn through a sagging door. My heart tiptoed nervously around inside me and my mouth was dry. I never was big on risk.

Hal led the way up rickety stairs into the barn loft which was filled with old trunks and boxes. The place smelled of mold and dust.

"Okay," I whispered fearfully. "You got us up here. Now what?" The barn creaked and sighed with the miseries of its age, and a chill skittered up my spine and into my hair.

"You see those trunks and stuff?" Hal asked. It was a dumb question. They were scattered everywhere. But he had to string out his little drama, so I nodded impatiently, more and more edgy. Perhaps a rabbit has the same sense of impending doom in a box trap just before the door falls behind him.

Hal, with the corny flair of a third-rate magician, threw back the lid of the nearest trunk. The first thing I saw was an Indian headdress. The feathers looked as if they had molted from a constipated owl, and the beadwork was old enough to have been done by a lady friend of Sitting Bull——but it still wasn't the kind of thing you'd expect to find in a loft.

The inside of the trunk lid had a name stenciled on it: "Hogan and Gunnison Road Shows." I don't know what Old Lady Gunnison's background was, but it must have had its romantic moments.

The headdress was creased flat from having been pressed in the trunk for years. I pulled it open and put it on. It was too big, but my large ears helped support it. My mother always compared me to Clark Gable, but my father told people I looked like a taxicab coming down the street with the front doors open.

We dived into the trunk, forgetting our fear in the flush of discovery. "Look at me!" Frank cried. He put on an evening gown and stuffed the bosom with old rags. He looked like a Wagnerian heroine as seen by Walt Disney.

Frank minced across the loft, contorting his face in what he imagined was hauteur. It looked more like gastritis. Hal and I doubled over, hanging on to each other for support. We rummaged through the trunk, looking for costumes to top Frank's.

"Hey, you guys! I'm a Chinese Indian!" I shouted. I wore a kimono and brandished a hatchet. I whirled to show them my creation and my heart leaped like a spawning salmon at a waterfall. Old Lady Gunnison was marching up the steps, and thunder and lightning detonated around her brow. It was like looking up to see a tyrannosaurus studying you and salivating. "Get out of here! You hoodlums!" Old Lady Gunnison brandished a lethal-looking cane like Stan Musial getting ready to face a rookie pitcher. "Get out of my barn!"

She advanced on me, swinging the cane. It swished through the air with the menacing whisper of Ben Hogan's no. 2 wood. I moaned in terror, tripped, and fell backward into the trunk. She towered over me, raising the cane high above her head. "No!" I cried. "Don't hit me!" I struggled helplessly to get out of the trunk.

"Leave him alone, you old bag!" Hal charged in and grabbed Old Lady Gunnison's arm. She turned on him with the charm of a rabid wolverine. The respite gave me just enough time to lurch out of the trunk and put a few feet between us. Not nearly enough. Enough would have been the distance between Birch Lake and Tierra del Fuego. I didn't much care which one of us was where as long as we were one at each place.

I backed in a wide circle. She made a little dash toward Frank.

I saw an opening and scooted past her. As she turned to intercept me, Frank and Hal leaped for the stairs. Our youthful speed barely beat her experience. Lord only knew how many bones of innocent (well *almost* anyway) children littered her property. Her heavy cane whispered past my ear. Then I was taking the steps three at a time. The half-open door seemed a thousand miles away.

"Come back here!" she snarled, hitching her skirts as she started down the steps after us. Fat chance! I'd sooner have stuck my ear in the wringer of my mother's washing machine.

As we sprinted toward the barn door, keening in terror, another event was shaping, one which would dovetail with our present low circumstance.

Elmer Blosser had been sitting in the bar, awash to the scuppers in beer, flabby gills reddened by alcohol, piggy eyes glinting with deep suspicion. He had been thinking about the stranger who'd gotten off the weekly bus that morning. The man looked neither tourist nor salesman. He carried no fishing rod, no sample case. He had been wearing a trench coat and his hat was low on his forehead. Of course, the early morning had been chilly and it was raining when Elmer saw the man, but the more beer Elmer drank, the more suspicious he became. Scenes from early Alfred Hitchcock movies flickered inaccurately through his fuddled brain. He imagined a bulge under the trenchcoat that only could have been a Luger or perhaps a bomb powerful enough to flatten Birch Lake.

"You can't tell me that ain't suspicious, that guy not havin' no luggage or nothin'," he growled. "Well, hell, what does *any*one do in Birch Lake if he don't fish?"

You had to admit, he had a point there.

"Wouldn't be surprised if he wasn't some red commie Nazi fascist!" Elmer grumbled, setting some sort of international record for jumbling political labels.

"Elmer," my Uncle Floyd said, wiping a beer glass, "what would a spy want in Birch Lake?"

"Lookin' for a place to hide a submarine pen, by God!" Elmer said, having given the matter considerable of what passed for thought with him. "I figure you could hide them damn things up in Cedar Lake where it's deep and run them out into the river at night and right up to Lake Superior. Sink every damn boat in the damn lake!"

My uncle stopped wiping, his lips pursed pensively. And then he caught himself and shook his head irritably. It was bad enough to have to listen to Elmer, but when you started believing it . . .

Elmer sucked down the better part of a glass of beer and brooded. "By God, I'm just gonna look into that feller," he said. He assassinated the beer expertly and slammed the glass down on the bar. He weaved toward the door, hitching up his gunbelt and belly. Visions of the Congressional Medal floated through his head, riding strong breezes of pure Bruenig's lager gas.

Elmer staggered slightly when the brilliant afternoon sunlight assaulted his watery eyes, but regained his balance and struggled heroically on. The stranger had walked——no *skulked*—— toward the south end of town, and Elmer turned that way.

It was as he was passing Old Lady Gunnison's house that he heard a blood-chilling shriek. "Hoodlums! Criminals!" Elmer stumbled to a halt, his peace officer's instincts struggling to disheveled attention. Instantly, he knew all. The stranger, festooned with vials of nitroglycerine and opium, had attacked poor Old Lady Gunnison and was going to white slave her.

Elmer lumbered through the front yard, tugging at his rusty pistol. He tripped over Old Lady Gunnison's prize Blaze Climber, destroying the trellis and scattering a regal shower of rose petals in his path. He staggered into the back yard and was greeted by an incredible sight.

We poured through the barn door in a bizarre eruption. Frank ran for his life, hitching up a swirling pink evening dress. A woman's hat, heavily feathered, lay low over his ears. From Old Lady Gunnison's vantage point, close behind us, he looked like a woman midget being attacked by a pheasant.

Hal's costume must have been the villain's in some weepy old melodrama. He wore a black suit, topped by a stovepipe hat, and a long, black cape billowed behind him. He looked like Count Dracula racing the sunrise.

I still had on the molting headdress and a kimono. I didn't even realize I was brandishing a blunt tomahawk as I fled for the all-too-distant woods. If a little bitty woman with a bird on her head and a diminutive vampire shook Elmer, the Oriental Indian really staggered him.

He recoiled and the enormous pistol went off with a deafening roar. His first shot was involuntary, but the buck of the pistol in his meaty fist kicked the key log out of all his pent-up hopes, dreams, frustrations, ambitions, and beer-soaked daymares. He was in battle at last. Anyone with a kimono had to be a Jap spy. The pistol boomed and jumped as he emptied it after us.

I was terror stricken. My breath rasped and my throat flamed. I realized that a persistent, almost supersonic keening I was hearing was my own voice, wailing in mordant harmony with the bullets singing overhead.

It was like one of those quicksand nightmares where you know something really ugly is about one-half jump behind you, bent on unzipping you from scalp to heel. The woods seemed to recede. The kimono flapped at my heels like a yapping feist, trying to trip me.

Hal always was a step faster than I was, especially when running from trouble. He darted into the trees and vanished like an exorcized spirit. An instant later, I ducked behind the first bush and corkscrewed through the sprouts with the panicky precision of a flushed woodcock.

After I put a hundred yards of thick underbrush between me and Elmer, I flopped exhausted in the grass, sucking in oxygen with ragged gasps. I trembled all over and my lips whuffled and fluttered like those of a nickering horse.

I heard a rustling in the bushes and got ready to run again. "Bobby? You here?" It was Hal. He stared at me with stricken eyes. "They got him!" he whined. "They got Frank!"

A spasm of fear turned me watery. "D——d——d——did he g——g——g——get shot!"

"I don't think so. He tripped over that crummy old dress and fell down. I heard him yelling after that."

"What're we gonna do?" I quavered.

"We got to get him back somehow," Hal said grimly. "He's my brother. My ma'd kill me if I come home without him."

Idiotically, my tottering brain paraphrased the famous Boys' Town motto: "He ain't heavy, Ma. He's locked up in jail."

"Let's sneak back and see," Hal said. We tiptoed back toward the barn. I realized I had the tomahawk and clutched it more firmly. It was better than nothing. We peered through the bushes and what we saw froze our sweetbreads. Elmer had Frank slung under his arm like a sack of hams while his still-smoking pistol dangled from the other hand.

He loomed over Old Lady Gunnison, and for a terrible moment we thought he had shot her. But then she scrambled to her feet, agile as a ferret. She had fallen over a decaying hog trough. She was slightly sprained, but too angry to feel pain. She hopped toward Elmer, screaming at him: "Get out of here! Get out of here! Get out of here!"

Somewhat repetitive, but the meaning was unmistakable, especially when she added, "Get off my land, you big drunk dungheap! I'll crack your thick skull!" In case Elmer missed the point, she snatched up an old two-by-four and crowhopped toward Elmer, who stood with his mouth open until he realized she meant to brain him. he took a last, petrified look, then turned and lumbered off. Frank jounced under his arm, forgotten.

"Lemme go!" Frank shrilled. "I ain't done nothin'!" Not strictly true, but it was no time to be picky.

"Quick!" Hal hissed at me. "Let's cut him off up at the corner. Old Elmer's headed for the jail." He turned and started to run. I followed him.

We sprinted through the edge of the woods, with branches slapping and grabbing us. When we cleared the woods, we ran across a small field and struggled up a steep bank to the cracked and heaved old sidewalk. We ran down it to the corner. I peeked around the hardware store and, sure enough, there was Elmer headed toward us. He was close to Uncle Floyd's bar.

"We gotta hurry!" I cried, turning to Hal. A crazy recklessness settled over me like a strange spell. We had done so much wrong that there was no reason for caution now.

We raced back along the hardware store, cut behind it, passed behind the grocery store and the Post Office, then burst through the back door of Uncle Floyd's bar. It was as if we had practiced this untamed charge a thousand times. We worked in perfect harmony.

Hal had his inevitable step on me again. He crashed through the screen door which banged explosively against the stacked beer cases. Bottles clattered and rattled. We thundered through the storeroom and into the main bar.

I don't know what devil possessed me then——maybe the sight of the drinkers frozen in midgulp——but whatever it was, it was exhilarating. An enormous smile split my face under the war bonnet and pure joy suffused me.

I screeched a war cry that would have turned Crazy Horse

green with envy. I brandished the tomahawk and howled, whooped, and roared. Hal shook his hands, sped through the bar yelling, "Over the top, boys! Let's get 'em!"

It was a strange moment.

Hal crashed through the swinging doors at the front of the bar with me a step behind. The timing was as smooth as a Swiss watch movement. Just as we burst out of the bar, Elmer lurched past the door.

I saw him start to turn, slack-jawed, but we had the twin elements of surprise and sobriety. I chopped at the pistol, still dangling from his hand, and he squawked and dropped it clanging to the sidewalk. Hal scooted around Elmer and grabbed his struggling brother by the ears, the only convenient (and prominent) handle, and began to wrestle Elmer for him. Elmer instinctively tightened his grip, but I hit him on the kneecap with my trusty, rusty hatchet, bringing forth a howl of pain.

He dropped Frank and Frank hit the pavement running like Harrison Dillard. We were on his heels.

I risked a quick glance behind and saw Elmer clutching his bruised knee and hopping ponderously. We vanished around the drug store and didn't stop running until we slipped through the hole at the back of the ice house. In the cool of the second floor we squatted anxiously, breathing heavily.

"We got to get an alibi," Hal said, as soon as he could talk. "Man, they could put us away for one hundred years!"

"I don't think old Elmer knew who we were," Frank said. He gnawed a vagrant fingernail nervously and frowned. A sprinkling of freckles tumbled into the creases on his forehead. "He kept saying something about spies."

"Spies?" Hall said. "What spies?"

"Heck, I don't know," Frank said. "I heard him say, 'By doggies, I got me one of them little bitty Jap spies. I'm gonna show them guys at the bar.'"

Hal shook his head. "Old Elmer's drunker than I thought."

"What about Uncle Floyd?" I asked. "He knows us."

We contemplated probable terrible punishments. "Well, let's get rid of this stuff anyway," Hal said. We took off the costumes and stuffed them under our shirts. Apprehensively, we slipped across the street at the far end of town, came through the woods to the little shack in back of the bar. We dropped the costumes down the contoured holes, peered outside, saw no one, and tiptoed to the back door of the bar. We carefully eased the door open and slipped into the storeroom.

"Spies! I tell you spies! Floyd, you know damn well they came out of here!"

"Elmer," said my Uncle Floyd. "I give you my word, I never sold a beer to a spy in my life. Honest to Robert Taft."

"Don't give me no fairy tales, Floyd," Elmer growled, peering suspiciously at my uncle. "You sure you ain't no damn New Dealer?"

"Have a brew, Elmer."

"I got to find them spies," Elmer said. But he didn't move and my uncle drew a frosty glass of beer, topping it with a creamy head. The foam overflowed and oozed down the sparkling side of the glass. Elmer licked his lips.

"Little bitty spies," he said. "They attacked that pore Old Lady Gunnison and then they tried to get me. I think I winged a couple up there in the woods. Soon as I get the pain out of my leg where they used a ray gun or something, I'm gonna go up there and find them bodies."

He drained the glass and banged it down on the bar top. Foam slid slowly to the bottom of the glass. "It was," he concluded, belching dramatically, "the goddamndist thing I ever seen!"

The next day Elmer went to Rice Lake and tried to enlist in the Marines. But he was too old (and too drunk). Uncle Floyd never did rat on us. Elmer told the tale time and time again to the awed farmers at the bar.

For the rest of the war, he was Birch Lake's expert on espionage.

UNCLE AL MEETS COUNT DRACULA

My cousin Hal was the first to spot the poster on the Birch Lake Rialto: "Huge Halloween Horror Festival!" it shrieked in blood-red letters. Garish typography promised us a glut of fright. Green ghouls threatened screaming maidens with venom-dripping fangs. Monsters lumbered, skeletons rattled.

My heart thumped. It was every kid's idea of pure entertainment——to have the pee wadding scared out of him for three hours.

The day before Allhallows was suitably spooky. Low-slung clouds scudded through a dead sky. The big old hemlock in my grandmother's yard hissed and moaned in the chill wind. Midday was as dark as late evening and thunder rumbled in the distance. A storm was brewing. Monsters stirred uneasily in their harsh crypts. We headed toward the Rialto and our heels clopped hollowly on the board sidewalk. Somewhere a dog barked, then howled. I swallowed noisily.

The Rialto, a tin-sided dump that looked as if it once had been a hangar for the Lafayette Escadrille, was filled with hyperactive adolescents, their pulses stuttering.

The first of the three movies opened on a misty, silent scene, filled with gnarled trees and strip-mine landscaping. There was a community sigh and the theater hushed. A sudden, eerie, chilling wolf howl filled the building, echoing off the tin sides, and the little hairs on the back of my neck leaped to attention like a battalion of frightened recruits. It looked like a really fine afternoon.

What followed were three hours of unremitting terror. I braced myself into the seat, knees jammed into the seat back ahead of me. Every nerve fiber was taut. Vampires flitted through tortured nights, deadly fangs exposed. Hands reached from dank graves to clutch the soft, white ankles of innocent girls. Mumbling mummies roamed the streets, seeking revenge for violated crypts. Lightning illuminated the wide-eyes faces of rapt kids in the audience. Monsters rose on the screen, amid a corona of short circuits and electrical arcs.

Oh, it was marvelous!

We left the theater, drained and shaken, and ran into Uncle Al, shambling by, a fishing rod in one hand, a nice string of brook trout in the other. He squinted a bloodshot eye at Dracula in full leer. "Looks like a guy from over to Haugen I bought a beer for last night," he growled.

Uncle Al was the family black sheep——hardly a strayed lamb——but an old, woolly, battle-and-bottle-scarred ram who bached in a couple of rooms at the rear of my grandmother's house. He was afraid of my grandmother (who wasn't?) but not enough to quit drinking beer, fishing and hunting. He still wouldn't chew tobacco in front of his mother and he still believed the fiction that she didn't know he drank beer.

"Cummon, Uncle Al," Hal said. "I bet you'd run just as fast as anybody if you met Dracula."

"Not 'less I owed him money," Uncle Al said. "I'd offer him a beer." He gave us a cavernous grin. He had forgotten his false teeth again.

"He don't drink beer," I said. "He drinks blood."

"Well, then that guy last night couldn'ta been Dracula. Not 'less blood's got a head on it." He guffawed and wandered off toward home.

"Uncle Al oughta know better'n to scoff," I said uneasily, my mind still filled with flitting spooks. "You know what happens to scoffers. They get stakes in their hearts with a gooshy sound or something." I hunched my shoulders to the ululating wind and the lowering sky.

We started toward home and I managed to kick a rock for two blocks before I lost it in the weeds. I looked up and there was the Mason Mansion. Every town has a Mason Mansion, a brooding Victorian shambles, vacant for years, squatting on a vast, unkempt tract of land surrounded by a wrought-iron fence. The Mason Mansion had broken windows, sagging doors, and shutters that canted crazily and creaked in the moaning wind.

Everyone said it was haunted. There were reports of flickering blue lights behind the musty, tattered curtains. Some had heard shrieks in the night, but admitted they could have come from a neighborhood peacock which was known to keep strange hours.

"Dare you to go in the Mason Mansion," Hal challenged.

"Not me. I dare you!"

It was a standoff. Neither of us wanted to admit he was scared, but neither of us wanted anywhere near that old tomb. "Let's both go in, then," I said. Frankly, I'd have been more confident had I been with John Wayne, but Hal was better than nothing.

We tiptoed to the door.

The wind scurried through the old house with a variety of moans guaranteed to make a little boy's breath come quick. The door sagged open at my tentative push, with a rust-ridden cry of pain. Dust and cobwebs lay over the high-ceilinged entryway. Something rumbled somewhere as we slunk, scarcely breathing, into the front room. Monster waking up in the dungeon? Smelling kidmeat? *"Let's get out of here!"* I squeaked.

And Hal tripped me.

He stuck his foot behind me and shoved and I tumbled over and he raced out the door and slammed it behind him and I was alone.

I leaped to my feet and ran to the door. Something rolled down the great staircase behind me. Thump! Thump! Thump! A head! Dripping blood? I wouldn't look. I screamed and jerked at the door, which wouldn't open. The wind howled and snarled through the house. There was an overpowering thunderclap and I sensed something just behind me.

The door suddenly gave and I flung it open and set a new world record for the five-block sprint.

"Lands!" my mother exclaimed. "You look as if you'd seen a ghost!"

Halloween Eve, the night when ghosts walk and monsters stalk. When I announced shakily that I didn't want to go trick-or-treating, my mother clapped a hand to my forehead and said I felt hot. If terror is warm, then I was hot. I was sure the Mason Mansion spooks now knew my name, address and telephone number and would seek me out that very night and settle my adolescent hash for scoffing. I knew scoffing was going to get me in trouble some day.

No superstitions plagued Uncle Al who announced he was going to "take a little stroll downtown," a euphemism meaning he was going to the tavern. My grandmother glared at him, but before she could say anything, he fled. My mother consigned me to bed. With feet of concrete, I dragged to my room at the back of the rambling old house. One window opened on a big, screened porch.

I didn't want to turn off the light, for I knew I would be threatened by Night Things, those corner-of-the-eye beasties who are never quite there when you look directly at them. My grandmother came back and turned off the light. "Wasting electricity," she declared. "Between you and Albert . . . ," and she left me in the dark. The dark dark. Geez, it was dark!

A full moon showed intermittently through rifts in the scudding clouds. A werewolf moon, as a matter of fact. Something crouched by the dresser, only it wasn't there when I slowly slid my eyes toward it. I swallowed and it sounded like a dozen marbles falling down a rainspout.

Somehow I fell into a fitful sleep, and then a dream began, filled with nightmare creatures who groped for me with scaly fingers. With a choking cry I came awake, my heart pounding. I lay rigidly in the grip of terror and something bumped in the back yard. There was a fluttering sound near the window. *Dracula!* screamed my mind. Fright turned my bones to water. They were after me. It was the Night of the Undead and they were coming for me. I lay there weak with fear and waited for the blood-lusting Count to come through the window and bare his incisors at me in a fateful grin. The moon washed dead light through the window.

There was a muffled thump against the house and my heart froze. Something scraped along the siding. Claws! I whimpered. The board on the porch step creaked and the night insects suddenly became silent. Then the screen door creaked. *Mom! Dad!* The words were shouts in my head, but I couldn't get any sound out. A step on the porch now. A shuffling, muted sound, like the shambling lurch of the Mummy Who Could Not Die! I imagined cerements shredding from a crypt-escaped cadaver, empty eyeholes seeking me out. A shadow fell across the window and I bleated in terror. The curtains billowed in. I heard hoarse breathing.

Then a shapeless figure loomed, blotting out the moonlight. It scrabbled at the window, lifted it, began to *enter my room*! I'd had enough.

"Yeeeeeeeeaaaaaahhhhhh!" I screamed loudly enough to wake any dead not already wandering around my room. My feet didn't touch the floor all the way to the hall. The window, one of those heavy, insecure old things with a bad habit of slamming shut, like a blunt-edged guillotine, came crashing down, and there was a gravelly, anguished scream as it trapped the Thing. I wondered briefly how a falling window could hurt a Thing. I thought it took a silver bullet or a stake through the heart. Mine was not to reason why . . .

I met my father halfway down the hall, tousle-haired and half asleep. I blubbered, gesturing and gurgling. "What's the matter? What's the matter?" he shouted, shaking me.

"Thing! Room! Window! Claws! Run! Wall! Couldn't! Big! Moon! Growl! Get!" It sounded as if I'd shaken my entire vocabulary in a bushel basket, then dumped it on the floor.

"Burglar? Prowler?" My father questioned, tossing a couple of words at me to see if they fit. I moaned and he took that for assent and ran to get his shotgun. I ran after him. He wasn't going to leave *me* alone. We tangled as I continued one way and he whirled to go the other. There was a moment of balletic confusion, then he knocked over a lamp and a chair. "For crying out loud!" he snarled. "Get out of the way!"

He charged down the hall. I don't think he intended to use the shotgun, but when he saw the shadowy figure wrestling with the window, he became excited and the gun somehow went off. There was an incredibly loud *"Bang!"* and plaster rained down from a crater in the ceiling.

All was confusion. Dracula, propelled by the proximity of no. 4 shot, jerked the window completely out of the frame, amid a shatter of glass and splintering wood. He then neatly took the screen door off at the hinges and vanished into the night, trailing screen wire and window framing.

Lights went on all over the house. "What was it? What was it?" My mother kept shouting. She had the idea it was an Indian attack, a legacy from her own childhood bedtime stories. My grandmother always put her children to bed with a good massacre.

"Prowler?" my father said. "Never heard of any prowlers in Birch Lake. Why in the world would anyone want to prowl in Birch Lake?"

Uncle Al appeared at breakfast the next morning and took no part in all the conversation about the intruder. He looked as if he had run through a basket of startled cats on the way home, but then that wasn't all that unusual for him, so no one commented on it.

I do know that he went on the wagon for awhile (about a week). Maybe it was him at the window, confused by good Wisconsin lager. Or maybe it was something from the Mason Mansion. Someone said that, when they tore down the Mansion, they found human bones, but that's all I ever heard. No one determined if the Mansion was haunted or just another sad old abandoned house.

However, it was a *long* time before I went to another spook movie.

MY FATHER'S MILLION-DOLLAR GARDEN

We all suffered when my father started his long-dreamed-of garden, but my mother really agonized because she was the family book-keeper and knew what it was costing.

When we quit the city for Birch Lake, it meant a big drop in income, but there were supposed to be compensations——the unfamiliar tang of clean air, bird whistles instead of braying ones from traffic cops, and having our own garden. "I'm going to have a garden you won't believe!" my father enthused.

That much, at least, proved to be true.

My father grew up on a farm, wearing a tattered pair of overalls and a rumpled hill-country grin. A rich residue of garden memories clung to his imagination through those long years in the city, and now that we were back in a small town those boyhood scenes came tumbling back like a troop of happy acrobats. Never mind that his mother had to work like a Russian peasant to make the thin soil cough up edible plants, nor that she had a flock of chickens and a few scrawny cows producing the world's greatest fertilizer.

"My mother used to use cow manure and grow tomatoes out of this world!" he exclaimed to my mother, looking at the weedy patch of bur-ridden sand he was calling his garden patch. My mother grimaced, as if she had eaten something that didn't agree with her. Perhaps it was something she heard.

After living with my grandmother until we found a place of our own, even the old wasp-ridden place we finally settled into seemed like a castle. Living with my grandmother was like being a buck private and having to bunk with Gen. Douglas MacArthur.

My mother was swabbing down the kitchen when the man showed up with the dump truck. "Is this where the dirt goes, lady?" asked the wind-scoured man. He was wearing a T-shirt, one-tenth grime and nine-tenths holes, and a barnyard redolency that made me long for a position far upwind.

"What dirt?" asked my bemused mother, who was trying to clean dirt *out*, not bring it *in*.

"Search me, lady," the man shrugged. "I got a load of topsoil supposed to go here." He waited expectantly, while my mother wrung her hands.

"Is my dirt here?" my father cried, bounding into the room. And the two of them trotted out to the sagging truck. My mother was aghast. "Got to get some good loam into that sand," my father confided during supper (the vegetables were skimpy grocery-store produce, limp and wistful).

"Don't you think it would be better to get established before we spend a lot of money on a garden?" my mother ventured.

"Nonsense!" my father thundered. "There's no more economical expense than a good garden, not to mention the health value. I'm tired of eating these pale little things with bug spray on them. I want healthy vegetables grown in healthy dirt!"

My mother raised her eyes as if invoking help from above, but perhaps she was looking at the ancient ceiling which threatened to collapse and induce serious skull fractures. We didn't have the money to repair it. My spinach, which I had thought was pretty good because Popeye told me so, suddenly tasted like bug spray.

My father bought a garden tiller. It cost $150 and it did two things——till the soil and make my mother's teeth grate audibly. "For Heaven's sake!" she exclaimed. "We can barely afford to pay the bills we have now and you spend that much on that——that——whatever it is!"

"It's a *tiller!*" my father cried, deeply injured. "Just the greatest gift to gardening that ever was. Just think, being able to till in organic stuff as much as eight inches deep!"

"I'd like to see it try to dig us out of debt," my mother muttered. "There's an organic trick it doesn't have in its mechanical brain."

There seemed to be a daily procession of things we couldn't afford. There were 10 bales of hay for the strawberry bed, then a truckload of wood chips for fruit tree mulch (the trees cost $8.50 each and looked like the switches my father cut to educate me with). "Of course I love your trees," my mother said with heavy sarcasm. "I have to——they cost as much as if they were my children."

"You're foot dragging," my father accused. "Doggone it, can't you have a little faith in me?"

"Faith!" my mother cried. "We're going broke! I have faith in enough money to pay our bills, that's what I have faith in. Not in mulch or trace elements or some silly thing that costs a hundred and fifty dollars and churns chicken manure! Why don't you plant a money tree?"

My father stormed out of the house, slamming the fragile screen door so hard it fell off the hinges. I'd never seen my parents bicker like this, and it frightened me. But my mother took a deep breath and later apologized, and they observed an uneasy truce.

I went with my father one Saturday afternoon to pick up a load of chicken manure. He had located a scruffy farmer who owned a flock of equally scruffy chickens and who hadn't cleaned out his chicken house since the year One.

"Nitrogen!" my father enthused, a little boy with a new toy. "Nothing better than chicken manure to put nitrogen in the soil!" I would have preferred to be playing second base for the Birch Lake Raiders, who hadn't won a game all year but at least didn't spend their hot Saturday afternoons scooping chicken manure into the bed of a decrepit pickup truck borrowed from my Uncle Al.

The farmer watched us grunting and straining as we scooped the acrid stuff, his face expressionless. When we were finished, the farmer flung aside a stalk of timothy he'd been chewing and said tersely, "That'll be ten dollars."

"*Ten dollars!*" my father exploded in outrage. "We cleaned

your lousy chicken house for you!"

The farmer shrugged. "Scoop 'er back in there then," he suggested. "Don't make me no difference. Don't make the chickens no difference either. Only makes you some difference."

My father plucked a very worn ten-dollar bill from his thin billfold and slapped it into the farmer's grimy hand. "Had to run into a rural Jesse James," he grumbled. A little later he cleared his throat and said, "I'd rather you didn't say anything to your mother about paying for the manure. She might not understand."

I was willing to bet on that.

And then the rabbits ate the pole beans. Each bean hill had its own application of well-rotted gunk and my father watered them as if they were rare orchids. As a result, the beans fairly shot out of the ground and soon were four inches tall, the best-looking plants in the garden. "You see!" my father cried. "It won't be any time until we're rolling in beans."

The next morning my father found that rabbits had discovered his little bean patch during the night and had devastated it. "Why me?" he shouted dramatically. "I can't even raise a lousy mess of beans!" I felt sorry for him.

He went downtown and bought 100 feet of chicken wire which cost $16 and six fence posts which cost another $18. He built a rabbit-proof enclosure. My mother spent one afternoon calculating how many cans of beans she could buy with $34.

"If we live to be two hundred years old," she told me bleakly, "I figure we might break even on this money-saving garden."

Then my mother discovered my father had bought a shredder for $95 without telling her. We happened to stop at the hardware store. "Really going in for gardening in a big way, eh?" commented Mr. Beldon who was unaware he was rubbing salt into a very tender wound.

"*I* certainly am not," my mother said stiffly.

"With that new shredder, your husband ought to be able to raise enough vegetables to feed the whole town." Mr. Beldon's grin sort of slid off the side of his face when he saw the expression on my mother's face.

"*What* shredder?" she asked, with a flat calm that made me gulp.

My mother was livid when we left the store. "That is absolutely the last straw!" she seethed. "I've put up with this foolishness long enough. He's going to save us money right into the poor house! Of all the thickheaded . . . ."

And so it went as we headed full ahead into a showdown that I didn't want. Visions of broken homes and crying children (me) filled my rattled mind.

My mother stormed into our ramshackle house, her eyes flashing. "Of all the silly, dumb things, this is the dumbest!" she ranted. The stove was lit and there was a pot of water steaming on it.

"Just like him!" she snarled, turning off the stove. "Run off and let the pot boil dry! Set the house on fire!" She trembled with fury.

My father bounded through the back door, the repaired screen door banging behind him. Dust motes eddied through the shafts of sun slanting into the kitchen. My father was holding a semigreen, knobby tomato. He jumped when he saw us.

He gestured hesitantly at a little pile of vegetables on the kitchen counter. They were the sorriest-looking things short of the city dump. There were five anemic carrots and a few limp pea pods and some thin bean pods and four small, careworn beets.

"I got some stuff out of the garden," he muttered haltingly, looking at my granite-faced mother. He swallowed and cleared his throat. "I was going to fix a stew for supper. With stuff from our own garden. I thought it would be kind-of nice . . . ." He trailed off and waved a vague hand. "There wasn't enough of any one thing," he said glumly. "So I was going to mix them all up in a stew."

He looked at the pitiful tomato as if it were a wart on his hand and said uncertainly, "I guess it wasn't such a good idea." I don't know if he meant the stew or the $400 garden. There was fatigue and disappointment and defeat on his face.

I wanted to hide because he was so defenseless. And because he was my father. I loved my tired, discouraged father.

"You were going to fix a stew? For us?" my mother said in a strangled voice. My father nodded, as if he were expecting a whipping. That's what I expected. He raised his head.

"Why, you're crying," he said wonderingly. "There are tears all over your face."

She sniffled and went to him and hugged him, pausing to wipe at her eyes. He looked at me over her shoulder, bewilderment creasing his forehead. "I just wanted to surprise you."

"Well, you always do that," she said severely and wiped her nose. She picked up one of the bloodless carrots, frowned at it, then looked at my father. "I've never seen a worse garden," she told him, but there was no rasp in the words. She shook her head in resignation. "I guess I'm just going to have to learn to put up with it."

I suppose when you love a person for his strengths, you have to love him for his weaknesses, too. Maybe that's what my mother meant. Anyway, things looked okay again.

They fixed supper together. Stew.

It was terrible.

A SUMMER ROMANCE

For most, a first romance conjures up sweet images of apple blossoms and moist hand-holding and fizzy sodas at the corner drugstore. But for me it brings up, like stomach gas, one dreadful day in July, a mammoth old road grader that looked like a gigantic, battle-scarred crab, and a classic whipping.

Margie still is vivid in my memory. But if I ever surface in hers, it is as a nightmare. I wonder what happened to her. She was lovely. I wonder if she ever thinks of me. Possibly. When things look really bleak in her life, when the kids are bickering and fighting and they all seem to be coming down with something, when she has a searing headache, when her husband gets off the commuter train after an extended session in the lounge car singing and staggering like Leon Errol (on the night the minister is due for dinner), it is then that I visualize her thinking to herself, "Well, it could be worse. I could have married what's-his-name up in Wisconsin."

I met Margie shortly after we moved to Birch Lake. My cousin

Hal knew her and it was he who brought us together for that fateful week of romance; that brief, soaring flight, so like that of the moth attracted to the searing flame. My flame was courtesy of the Elk County Highway Department.

Margie was a year younger than I. At 11, she was a watch-fob Debbie Reynolds, a pre-adolescent Sandra Dee. She made Annette Funicello look like Grandma Moses.

Hal had been courting (perhaps "running with" would be more accurate, since there was no motive involved more romantic than a good game of kick-the-can) a tomboy named Dorothy who came with her parents from Beloit each summer. This time she brought a friend, Margie, and Hal had met her. "She ain't bad for a girl," he said grudgingly, the highest possible praise. So, if I wanted to run around with Hal, who wanted to run around with Dorothy, then I would have to run around with Margie. I had little knowledge of girls, except that they couldn't throw out Rip Van Winkle at first on a hot grounder, assuming they even could field the thing, which I doubted.

Hal introduced me: "This is Bobby, my cousin," he said, with the manner of someone lecturing on the skeletal structure of an ugly insect.

Margie looked at me and smiled a 1,000-watt smile and I was lost, enveloped in a swirling fog of aching confusion, a frontal system of unidentifiable longing, a windstorm of love. She hit me harder than the little honey blonde who had sat one row over and three seats up in the fourth grade and who, I had been certain, was the great love of my life.

I gaped at Margie with slack-jawed love as I stumbled along beside her, looking, I am sure, remarkably like Mortimer Snerd.

"I used to live in Chicago," I blurted. "Our suitcase came apart when we moved up here and my mother's underwear got run over by an Allied moving van and my teacher said I ruined our school play nearly single-handedly last year."

She was confused, for which I couldn't blame her a bit. "You did what?" she asked, her brow furrowed as delicately as fine corduroy. I explained how I had gotten my finger caught in the scenery and how all the settings had collapsed, followed almost instantly by my teacher, Miss Allendale.

She laughed, a sound like an angel's violin. She was my Snow White and I was her Seven Dwarfs. I looked most like Dopey as I shambled in her delicious wake.

Hal and Dorothy turned in at Bamberger's Grocery where we bought our ice cream cones. I fished a quarter from my threadbare jeans (the first one I'd had all summer) and told Mrs. Bamberger, "Give me a double-dipper."

I looked at Margie. "We can share it," I said masterfully. Then the daring of such a proposal left me weak all over, the way I'd been when I was fresh from chicken pox. The sudden thought that her tender lips would touch the same ice cream as mine reduced me to lifeless ashes. I glowed and sputtered, a defective wick of rapture.

We left the store and Hal led the way to the old town ice-house, our hideout in time of strife and, in this case, in time of tranquillity. We sat in the cool damp to enjoy our cones. I watched, fascinated, as Margie's pink tongue traveled around the dripping side of the cone, deftly sweeping off the rivulets of melting ice cream.

"Here," she said. "It's your turn."

I nipped a delectable mouthful from the pointed top and let it dissolve blissfully in my mouth, then handed it back to her. We all relaxed and watched the summer day drone past. Through the loading door opening, we looked out from cool sanctuary as the summer sun burned down on dusty weeds and old dogs lay painfully in slender shade. A wasp hovered in the door like a tiny helicopter, then tilted and vanished outside. It was the happiest day of my life.

Margie and I swam together that week. We talked and walked together and shared countless ice cream cones. The stock of small change, carefully hoarded in a Prince Albert can under my mattress, steadily depleted, but I didn't care. I even laid out 20 cents and bought her a chocolate soda.

"Margie," I said in the middle of that week. We were walking past the lumberyard and the smell of fresh-sawn pine mingled delectably with that of road tar.

"Yes?" She looked at me, honey hair glinting in the hot sun.

"Margie, I like——I mean——you know——you."

She smiled an easy, happy smile. "I know," she replied. "Me too."

I was overcome. I found an advertisement for friendship rings in an old confessions magazine that belonged to my Aunt Helen. The rings came twined together, like snakes (though I think it was clasped hands), but could be separated and worn by each party to romance.

My mother resolutely refused to give me $4.98 to buy the rings and I howled in rage. Didn't she understand at all what was important? Didn't she have any sympathy, any love at all for her only child? I swore passionately I'd earn the money somehow and seal the eternal bond between my darling and me.

So involved was I that I scarcely could bear it on Thursday when Margie went shopping somewhere with Dorothy and her mother. Hal and I floated aimlessly around Birch Lake as we had done in the days before Love walked in. We watched a couple of games of snooker at Kelly's Pool Hall, played catch behind my grandmother's shed, and went swimming at the dam.

On our way back to town after swimming, we saw Ed Ferguson returning home from work on his big county road grader and we waved at him. He stopped the machine and leaned out. "Want a ride?" he shouted over the growl and thump of the old engine. He motioned us to the ladder-like steps leading to the cab and we scrambled up. We were wide-eyed with excitement. He grinned at our obvious pleasure and put the monster in motion, slapping levers and stamping pedals with his hands and feet in professional harmony.

To make the moment perfect, we passed Margie and Dorothy just coming out of the grocery store. I shouted and waved. Margie waved back and I saw her talking excitedly with Dorothy's mother and pointing at me. My pride was boundless.

That's the way the week went, in sunshine and happy splendor. We talked extensively about nothing. We collected a healthy layer of dust playing hard, slept hard at night. Margie filled my days. Ah, it was a time of wonder and beauty. Then came that day I will never forget.

Margie and I decided to go to Bamberger's for a dessert ice cream cone after supper. The evening was cool and still. Sounds floated on the clear air from far away, a sign of probable rain before morning. We clearly heard the whining of the big saws in the lumbermill a mile away and, even farther, a motorboat on the lake. Somewhere a screen door creaked and slammed. It still was light, but the day was quiet and cooling from its earlier intense heat. The low sun shot searchlights from behind a dark mass of thunderclouds on the horizon.

We walked through town, got our cones, then went up the big

hill on the west side of Main Street, licking and talking. Ed Ferguson's road grader was at the top of the hill where he always liked to leave it. Positioned thus, it was an equally brief walk for him to his house or to the tavern, depending on what kind of day it had been.

We scuffed along the sidewalk, which was veined with frost fractures and chipped along the edges. "I rode up on that grader the other day," I said. "It was great."

"I saw you," Margie said. "You sure were up high. I was with Dorothy's mom."

"I saw you when you saw me," I answered intelligently. The conversation was beginning to sound silly, even to me, so I changed the subject. "I bet I could just drive that big old thing," I boasted as we drew even with the grader. "C'mon, let's climb up on it."

"You'd better not," Margie said. "You'd really get in trouble if they caught you."

I had seen Ed head for the tavern when he quit for the day and knew there was no chance he would see me. Once inside the bar, Ed glued himself to a stool and stayed there until pried loose late in the evening by my Uncle Floyd, who owned the bar. No one else was around. I couldn't resist the chance to impress my dove.

"If you won't, I will," I said. I went over to the old machine which appeared to be constructed of equal parts of yellow paint and rust. The wheels canted severely to one side as if the grader were trying to collapse. I reached to the second step and hauled myself up. I climbed into the cab and slipped onto the old leather seat which was cracked and seamed like a mud flat in a drought. Seat stuffing oozed here and there. It was dark and cool inside the machine and, as I looked down at Margie, she seemed small and far away. Stale pipe tobacco, sweat, and road oil mingled in the cab in acrid, not unpleasant disharmony.

"Want to see me drive her?" I called down teasingly.

"You get down from there, Bobby!" Margie piped. "You'll get in bad trouble!"

Her worried expression egged me on. She was impressed; no doubt about it. Experimentally, I twisted the big steering wheel, leaning on it to make it move. I made a noise like a motor: "Brrrroooommmmm, rrooooommmmmmmm," I growled.

I kicked the pedals in front of me and dealt a stiff blow to a couple of the levers, just as I had seen Ed do. To my utter consternation, the biggest lever flipped forward with an ominous click. When I tried to pull back on it, I couldn't budge it.

The machine lurched slightly and Margie squealed, "It moved! It's moving!"

Transfixed, I looked down at her. I saw her fading away behind me and thought she was backing off. But then I realized (great skittery mice of terror lurched crazily through my nervous system) that the *machine* was moving, not Margie. Quickly, the grader gathered speed on the sharp incline toward town. By the time I could react and start thinking about getting off, the monster was going too fast to risk it.

Of all the horrible things I had done since birth, this was the worst. They all reeled past my mind's eye and I held them up for comparison with the present mess and, no doubt about it, this was the worst. This was reform school stuff. My heart thundered with panic. My throat dried and my tongue welded to the roof of my mouth. I hummed with terror and thought awful thoughts.

"You're gonna get it. You're gonna get it. You're gonna get it. . . ." The phrase tumbled through my jumbled mind like a crazed acrobat.

I grabbed the wheel which jumped and shuddered under my hands with life born of movement pulsing up the steering column. I peered through a windshield so dirty as to defy vision. By now I was halfway down the hill and the grader was traveling faster than a road grader is designed to go. Vibrations thrummed up the steering column into my arms. I held the wheel in a death grip, an analogy that, when it occurred to me, made me whinny like a spooked horse.

I saw people running in front of me, scattering out of my way. As I sailed past the first of them, I saw faces turned up, mouths open. Normally, a road grader makes a great deal of noise, but because the engine was not running, I heard tatters of comment as I stampeded past.

"Hey, kid," yelled one man severely, "get off of there!"

"Stop him!" someone shouted.

"What you want me to do——get down in front of it?" was the derisively shouted answer.

One man caught up with me and grabbed the lowest rung of the ladder leading to the cab. His knuckles were white with the strain of holding on and I noticed sweat on his upper lip as he valiantly tried to vault up. But the speed of the machine was too great. He couldn't gain enough momentum to swing aboard and finally was forced to let go and jump aside before the huge rear wheel flattened him.

We rumbled onto Main Street, the grader and I, making the slight curve with surprising skill. I had learned quite a lot about driving a road grader on the trip downhill. Driving, but not stopping. There were screams. Birch Lakers gawped wide-eyed as I careered past.

I threaded my way down Main Street, but, distracted by the stress of learning road grader technique on the job and without an instructor, I failed to allow enough room between me and Harry Thompson's ladder.

Harry, the village house painter, was adding the finishing touches to a masterful job on the front of Beldon's Hardware Store and was looking forward to calling it a day and joining his old buddy Ed Ferguson for a cool one at Uncle Floyd's bar. Engrossed in his endeavors, he was unaware of me bearing down on him. The elevated grader blade just nicked the edge of his ladder. Harry was catapulted through the air and onto the front awning of the store where he clung desperately, wondering what in the hell had hit him.

One bucket of paint described a great arc and swiped a vivid scarlet streak across the stark white front of the Town Hall, next door. The other bucket was suspended like a hummingbird for a long instant. Then it slowly tipped as it fell and sluiced its contents over the head of Mr. Beldon, who had just stepped out of his store to see what was going on. A split second later, Harry fell through the awning on top of Mr. Beldon and the two of them crashed through a display of lawn furniture and rose trellises.

The grader pounded on. I had no choice but to follow the road. I didn't have the faintest idea how to stop the thing. A corner loomed. The road bent sharply, curling down to the dam at the end of Birch Lake. I began to cramp the big steering wheel for the turn and my blood chilled as I saw a car backing laboriously into a parking space, nearly blocking the road. There was no way I could miss it if I continued around the corner. I spun the wheel the other way and crunched straight ahead, across the curb and into a driveway.

The machine rumbled up the narrow driveway and squeezed past a garage, nicking off some siding with the right wheel. A clothesline snapped under the charging beast and a pair of capacious longjohns sailed over the cab and vanished behind me.

The grader blade leveled two apple trees, a lilac bush, and four blossom-laden rose bushes. A concrete birdbath went end for end and an indignant robin sputtered into the air in front of me.

Ahead lay the lake. I was trapped. Everywhere but in front there were big trees and outbuildings that herded me inexorably toward the dark waves of the deep water. The machine pounded and vibrated with its accumulated speed. I still had no idea how to stop.

I rumbled out on a spit of land a hundred yards from the water's edge. Any way I turned now, I would plunge over the steep bank and into the roiling waters. I began to cry. I pulled frantically and witlessly at the levers and knobs which jutted out everywhere in the cab.

The lake edge was closer. There was a drop of a dozen feet to the deep water. The hungry whitecaps licked the shore in anticipation. All that stood between me and the chill depths was the Peterson outhouse, a weathered structure set fashionably down a little gravel path lined with bright marigolds. I thought perhaps if I ran into it, I would stop short of the lake, so I altered course and bore down on it.

And then, to my utter horror, I saw someone inside, bustling about like a hen preparing its nest.

I shouted a warning, feeble and unheard. In blind terror, I jerked at the levers, now only feet from the little building. The door flew open and Alf Peterson peered out, warned of something amiss by the muted rumbling of the mighty engine of destruction as it zeroed in on him.

His eyes widened, first in uncomprehending surprise, then in fright. Again I pulled desperately at the levers with all my pitiful strength.

There was a jarring "clunk!" and the ponderous blade dropped. It bit instantly into the cool, green back lawn of the Peterson house and I was propelled painfully and violently forward against the windshield as the grader plowed up a tidal wave of dirt that flowed forward to engulf Alf in his little house, tilting them backward over the bank and into the lake.

Shaking like an aspen, I clambered down from the now-recumbent machine in time to be surrounded by the crowd that had formed behind me as I sped down the hill.

"You damn fool kid!" cried Ed Ferguson, puffing up to me. He whoofed for air. He was out of shape, not used to chasing his machinery. From the lake below came an inarticulate roar of rage as

Alf Peterson rose from the depths, like an overalled Poseidon. Had he been carrying Poseidon's trident, I'm sure he would have gigged me like a carp.

I started crying heavily, and I think the sight of my obvious misery saved me from some violent punishment. The crowd was in an ugly mood when it first arrived but couldn't bring itself to attack a skinny, crying little kid.

In the midst of all the explanations and confusion, I looked through tear-washed eyes directly into the face of my beloved Margie.

She stared at me with the same wary, shuddery fascination one shows a caged timber rattlesnake. I knew instantly the romance was over.

It took several days for the repercussions to die down. When I was able again to go out in public without utter shame and could reflect quietly in private on everything without cringing, I quietly destroyed the advertisement for the friendship rings.

GRANDMA AND THE BUCK DEER

Most kids try smoking. They get caught, get a whipping, or get sick and that's it. But before I finished my initial venture with the Weed, my grandmother hated me, my Uncle Al nearly committed multiple murder, my parents were ready to put me up for adoption, and the Wisconsin Department of Natural Resources and the Society for the Prevention of Cruelty to Animals could have put me away for life.

If my father hadn't been born in tobacco country, I'd probably be a smoker today, worrying about deadly respiratory diseases. The worry would lead to that gnawing craving for a cigarette. The cigarette would lead to more worry about smoking too much.

But I never touched a cigarette after the deer attacked my grandmother.

When we lived in Chicago, we were midway between Birch Lake and the gullied hills of Chariton County, Missouri. My father delighted in taking the products of one region to the other——

mixing the cultures like some erratic anthropologist. He'd take enormous, smelly cheeses from Wisconsin to Missouri where my paternal grandfather would take time out from shooting squirrels through the eyes with an ancient Winchester .22 to moan with delight as he wolfed them down.

In exchange, my father took such items as head cheese to Wisconsin. The first time he took head cheese, one of my Wisconsiner aunts, thinking head cheese was a form of dairy product, ate some with relish, and then, when told it was a mixture of hog brains, seasoning, etc., became violently ill.

My father's penchant for adulterating pure cultures is what led him to take a stick of tobacco from Missouri to Wisconsin.

It was homegrown burley. My Missouri grandfather had planted the tiny seeds early in the spring. He nurtured them through adolescence under cheesecloth, dug the plants, separated them, punched them in with a dibble, hand-hoed them, suckered them, picked off the tobacco worms, batted the mature moths out of the air with a flat paddle like Hank Greenberg hitting home runs, cut the stalks and hung them in the weathered old barn to cure, stripped the leaves, and twisted them onto a sharp stick which had been in our car trunk when we moved to Birch Lake.

My father hung the stick of tobacco in my grandmother's shed and we all forgot about it. That is, we all forgot about it except me and I remembered it one day as my cousins, Hal and Frank, and I were walking down the roadside ditch toward my grandmother's house. We had just suffered with Mr. Ken Maynard through a particularly hazardous plains epic.

"I bet you guys couldn't guess in a million years what my dad brought to to Grandma's," I challenged.

"Some more of them hog guts?" asked Frank in disgust. It was his mother who had become ill after eating the head cheese.

"That wasn't hog guts," I said. "And that isn't even close."

"Guess, guess, guess!" Hal exclaimed. "We always got to guess. Maybe we don't even care."

"Okay," I said, shrugging. "If you don't care."

"If you don't tell," Hal said, "I'm gonna introduce you to my knuckles." He gave me a look that would cure warts.

"Tobacco," I said promptly. "My dad brought a big bunch of home-grown tobacco from my grandpa's house down in Missouri. Bet you guys wouldn't smoke *that* stuff."

"What's so great about that?" Frank asked. "We tried smoking. It wasn't all that much."

"Yeah," I sneered. "But that was just cigarettes. *Anybody* can smoke cigarettes. My dad says this stuff will blow your sinuses halfway across a good-sized room."

"There ain't nothing *I* wouldn't smoke," declared Hal. "Bring on your rusty old tobacco."

We split up for lunch and promised to meet by the highway department storage shed at one o'clock. The garage was a wondrous place of hot tar smells and huge rusty equipment.

Right after lunch, I paid a visit to the shed where the tobacco was hanging. I cast a quick look at the house where I knew my mother and grandmother were baking. It was a scary moment. Mothers have a sixth sense which tells them when their children are doing something wrong. And I was convinced my grandmother could see through walls like Superman.

I slipped into the shed like a ghost with too many ribs showing. It was hot inside and I wasted no time in filching a twist of tobacco off the stick. I held it behind me and peeked out the door. No one. I eased outside, hiding the tobacco with my body. Once in the weeds at the end of the lot, I breathed more easily.

I followed the railroad tracks until I was safely out of sight of the house, then cut back toward town and the highway garage. Hal and Frank were already there, waiting impatiently.

"I got some matches," Hal said, showing a handful of the big old kitchen matches which popped like firecrackers when you lit them. Frank had nipped some cigarette papers somewhere.

"We better not smoke here," Frank said. "We might get caught."

"Let's go out toward the city dump," Hal suggested, ever the planner and idea man. "There ain't likely to be many people out there."

The suggestion had merit as long as we stayed upwind of the dump which, in those days before emphasis on civic sanitation, wasn't exactly a field of phlox. If high heaven was straight up, then the dump smelled to there, for it was located in an old gravel pit about a half mile from town and the aroma generally rose straight up, as if fired from a massive howitzer. It was enough to bring down passing airplanes.

We followed the tracks toward the dump which abutted them

in a patch of dense forest. When we got to the dump, we found the wind blowing up and across the tracks. "Whooey!" Hal exclaimed. "That's enough to stink a dog off a gut wagon!" It was a phrase he'd picked up from Uncle Al, an earthy type. I hadn't heard it and whooped with laughter. Hal looked pleased.

We left the tracks, slithered down the cindered embankment, and followed a dim trail through the woods around the dump until we had ourselves between the wind and the garbage. We tumbled into a pleasant little woodland glen, safe from prying eyes.

"Come on," Frank said impatiently. "Get the tobacco out." I brought out the twist and they watched me with bright eyes, thoughts of forbidden pleasures dancing like sinful sugarplums in their heads. We crumbled the brown leaves into our cigarette papers, spilling about three times as much as we salvaged.

Hal demonstrated how to roll a cigarette. It was a feat he had learned by watching the bad guys in the Saturday western matinees. There was about an inch of usable cigarette when he finished. It had long twists of paper on either end. It looked like a double-ended ladyfinger firecracker.

We finally made three cigarettes, each with a few puffs in them. We lit up. I dragged without inhaling, trying not to show that I wasn't enjoying that wonderful smoke all the way to my heels.

A certain heady feeling, a mounting pressure in my skull pushed out behind my eyeballs. It was as if someone were running wind sprints across my brain.

"Hey," I said. "That's really great, isn't it?" My enthusiasm was the same I would have shown an offer to sew my eyelids shut.

Frank whooped into a fit of coughing. He turned red and purple before our startled scrutiny. Alarmed, we pounded him on the back and looked anxiously into his brimming eyes. Finally he recovered somewhat, breathing raggedly. "I sure wouldn't walk no mile for *that* stuff!" he wheezed fervently.

"You already have," I pointed out. I was feeling queasy and lightheaded and I crushed the cigarette out on the forest floor.

It was then that I saw the big buck standing on the other side of the clearing looking steadily at us. His rack of velvet-covered antlers looked as massive as those of an elk. His shiny nose was startlingly black, his brown eyes steady and thoughtful. I thought I was seeing things. I thought the cigarette had brewed up a hallucination. But then I realized there really was an enormous, unafraid, and wild deer within 20 feet of me.

I grabbed for the other two, trying to hush them so they wouldn't frighten the animal.

But there was no danger of that. Obviously the buck knew we were no threat to him, at least nothing he couldn't handle with one hoof tied behind him. He was considerably more calm than I was. Paralyzed with wonder, we watched as the deer advanced across the clearing. He kept one eye on us, alert for any unfriendly move. He whistled noisily through his nostrils. With no hesitation, the buck picked up my twist of tobacco and chewed off a big chunk of it. He munched blissfully on it as my mouth fell open.

I was so astounded at the sheer effrontery of the animal that I jumped up and shouted, "Hey! You dumb deer!" The buck wheeled and sprang easily to the other side of the clearing, then turned and looked back at me.

I picked up the mangled tobacco twist and peered fearfully at it. I had a sudden vision of the tobacco poisoning the deer, then the game warden finding out how the deer had died and tracing the whole thing back to me. I didn't know until years later that deer easily can become addicted to the taste of tobacco and will go to extraordinary lengths to get it.

The buck pawed the ground and snorted, then tossed his antlers at us. He acted peeved——no, more than that. Pugnacious.

For the first time, I began to be a little apprehensive. Maybe the tobacco had made him crazy. Maybe he was rabid. The deer looked piercingly at the tobacco I was holding. It appeared that he regarded it as his property and was prepared to fight for it.

Frank and Hal were holding my arms and urging me to run. I needed time to think and didn't have it.

"C'mon!" Hal hissed. "That old deer looks mean!"

"Maybe he's got rabies!" Frank whined, voicing the scary thought that had been howling around in my head like a banshee. We began to edge away and the deer followed us, matching our every step. We backed all the way to the railroad embankment and up it. The deer was right behind us all the way and trotted along below us almost to the city limits before he turned and, with one last lingering look, melted into the woods.

"Whew!" Frank breathed in relief. "I thought that old buck was gonna get us!"

It was only then that I realized I still carried the hank of tobacco. All I needed was to trot into the house with a handful of the deadly weed. I threw it down and brushed the crumbs from my hands. I discovered I was trembling. The deer had looked as big and snake-mean as a tyrannosaur. He didn't remind me at all of Bambi. More like King Kong.

My mother thought I was coming down with something that night at supper. When my father lit a cigarette after dinner, I nearly threw up.

I went to bed early and lay there, my innards churning like a river in spring runoff. I finally fell asleep, but was awakened sometime in the middle of the night by an urgent need to visit the little structure located to the rear of Grandma's house.

I rose in the silence of the house and padded outside. The night was softly warm, one of those midsummer nights when the stars seem to have been taken down and polished, then put back up. As I passed my grandmother's shed, I noticed that the door was ajar. Absently, I pushed it shut and heard the latch on the outside click into place. I continued to my appointment.

On my way back to bed, as I passed the shed, I heard heavy breathing behind the closed shed door. *Ghosts!* I thought in terror. I sprinted for the house, whining in panic. The night, so soft and gentle, had turned to cat screams and wolf howls. I was utterly certain something was racing after me, poised to spring on my back and sink gleaming teeth into me. I skittered through the house and dived into my bed where I trembled and shook under the covers. Eventually, when nothing followed me into the house, I fell into a troubled sleep.

We were sitting at the breakfast table the next morning when we heard my grandmother shout. Most women would have screamed, but my grandmother wouldn't have screamed if Frankenstein's creature had invaded her kitchen. She'd have belted him in the electrodes with a frying pan.

Still, a shout from my grandmother indicated serious trouble and we all raced for the door to the back yard. My Uncle Al reached it first and already was galloping in his gimpy, arthritic fashion across the back yard when I ran out on the porch.

"What's goin' on, Momma! What's the matter?"

My grandmother was leaning against the shed door looking, for the first time since I had known her, somewhat nonplussed.

"There's a great big buck deer in there!" she exclaimed in a tone of utter disbelief. "I think he's eating my washing!"

Her incredulous outrage would have been funny except for two things: First, I had a flash of prescience. I knew exactly how that deer had gotten in there. It had followed the faint tobacco trail to the shed and I had shut him in the preceding night. The entire story must never, *never* come out or I might just as well go right down to the lake and jump off the dam. And I couldn't swim.

Second, this was my grandmother, beside whom Charles de Gaulle and Winston Churchill were wishy-washy old women. If she ever found out I was behind or had anything to do with the problem, she undoubtedly would insist that my mother put me up for adoption. And I wasn't sure my mother wouldn't do it.

Uncle Al, the family renegade, whose idea of hell was a place without hunting, fishing, and beer, shouted, "Hold him, Momma! Let me get my gun!" He sprinted back across the yard, colliding with my father in midsprint. They both went to earth dazed, but Uncle Al, his blood lust aroused by the thought of a trapped deer (and one that represented enough venison to satisfy his fondness for deer chili), scrambled to his feet and pounded into the house.

He was back in a flash, his old Winchester in one hand, a handful of coppery bullets in the other. He dropped them all over the porch in his haste to jam them into the loading gate on the side of the receiver.

"Hold him, Momma!" he shouted again. Uncle Al pursued deer with religious fervor (or perhaps irreligious fervor, considering he often hunted early on Sunday morning, maintaining that there was far less competition from other hunters whose "ball and chain had them tied to a church pew"). Normally he abided reasonably well by the game laws. Had he met a deer in the woods out of season, he would have passed in peace. But never before had a deer come right up to his house begging to be taken. It was too much for him.

Feverishly, he levered a shell into the chamber and raced across the yard. "Move aside, Momma! I'll let him out and we'll drop him!"

"Don't shoot him!" I yelled at the top of my voice, stung by an impulse which I instantly regretted. So loudly had I shouted that everyone stopped. My uncle turned, thinking momentarily that I was the game warden.

As all eyes turned on me, I felt I had to make some explanation and I sealed my destiny by blurting, "He's just after the tobacco.

Eating it. I mean, he doesn't. . . ." Here, I faltered and ground to a halt like a cheap clock——one whose time has run out.

My grandmother's face was quite a lot like that of Theodore Roosevelt on Mt. Rushmore, only not as pleasant. Storm clouds played around her granite brow. She looked across the yard at me and for a single, dreadful instant I felt her zoom to Olympian proportions. All I saw was her flinty, uncompromising face, as huge as the Lincoln Memorial, as awesome as King Kong knocking down the gate of his island prison. Utter comprehension flickered across her iceberg eyes.

She knew! Oh, God! She knew I was behind the whole thing. She began a steady march across the yard to where I cowered beside my mother. I seemed to hear rolling drums. I wanted to crouch behind my mother's skirt, shut my eyes, and yell in fear, but I just stood there with my mouth open, eyes wild as those of a range mustang feeling his first saddle.

Uncle Al had no time for whys. He didn't care for hows. He just wanted 200 pounds of unprocessed venison. He bounded toward the shed and all hell broke loose.

The buck, frenzied by fear at all the commotion, leaped at the door, kicking it. Just as Uncle Al reached the door, it burst open, catching him squarely in the nose. He went over backward, tears streaming. The gun exploded and there was a metallic "pang!" as the bullet went into the block of his ancient pickup.

The buck charged through the open shed door, right across Uncle Al, and headed for what looked like open country. Unfortunately, my grandmother had advanced to a point precisely between the buck and what the buck considered open country. The fear-crazed animal bore down on Grandma from the rear.

Both my mother and prostrate Uncle Al shouted a warning and my grandmother turned. As she whirled, the deer reached her. With fantastic reactions for a woman of her age, she grabbed the buck by his antlers and hung on grimly. She backpedaled nimbly as the animal reared and plunged, snorting and wondering what in the name of hell had him by the horns.

I had a vision of the deer carrying her off to the woods forever. It was uncharitable, but there was a tiny flicker of hope that such an event would solve my mounting problems.

"Leggo of him, Momma!" Uncle Al shouted. "I can't shoot!"

"I *can't* let go, you fool!" my grandmother snapped. "The beast is crazy!"

The buck was snorting like the town mill whistle and was trying to shake loose my determined grandmother. She held his head down so he couldn't use his hooves and danced in front of him as he plowed her along by brute strength. Uncle Al raised his gun, aimed and then lowered it helplessly. "Ah, Momma!" he cried in anguish. "Dammit! Hold still! I can't hit the thing with you movin' like that!"

Even in her desperate plight, she threw him a look that could have shriveled asbestos. "I'm——not——doing——this——for—— fun——you——dunce!" she snarled as she jounced painfully with the tossing of the buck's head. At that instant, they foxtrotted past the pickup truck and my grandmother, glimpsing a slender chance at safety, let go and clambered with the agility of a mountain goat onto the hood.

The buck, now more enraged than terrified, charged after her. As he tried to scale the hood of the Chevy, Uncle Al cut down on him. Unfortunately for the already seriously wounded old truck, Uncle Al's intentions were more direct than his aim. Another bullet ripped through the engine, laying waste to cylinders, valves and assorted intricate General Motors mechanisms.

"Put that gun down, you fool!" my grandmother howled as Chevrolet shrapnel whirred through the air around her. The buck, seeing he wasn't going to get Grandmother, returned to his original objective of putting a lot of distance behind him.

He headed for the front yard, soaring gracefully as only a deer can. Uncle Al gimped behind him, levering another round into the Winchester. As the deer nipped around a corner of the house, Uncle Al fired again. He missed, but the front window of the house across the street disappeared in a welter of flying glass. Undaunted, Uncle Al chased the buck into Grandma's front yard and shot again, just as the buck leaped across the road.

The bullet punched through a mailbox with a cymbal-like "clang!" and the little red flag popped up. Delivery today. The buck sailed across the blacktop just ahead of an oncoming car. The startled driver wrenched his steering wheel to the left, jounced into the ditch, then out on the road again. He hit a car whose driver had his entire attention fixed on Uncle Al because he thought my uncle was shooting at him.

The two cars collided with a grinding crash and the drivers immediately leaped out of them and began cursing each other.

Except for the impassioned oratory of the drivers, silence returned to the summer morning. I stood in the back yard, dread sifting down over me, like dust after an especially ugly explosion.

Everyone save my grandmother and me had followed the flow of action into the front yard——she because she was winded and me because the enormity of the situation and my guilty knowledge of it had me gluily congealed like a poorly conceived pudding.

She slid down from the hood of the murdered truck and stood beside it, trying to regain both her breath and her monolithic composure. She looked up, took a deep breath that nearly evacuated the oxygen from the yard, and beckoned to me. It looked like the finger of the Grim Reaper. With feet of pig iron, I approached her.

"How did that deer get in my shed?" she demanded in a measured, reverberating voice which easily could have been coming from the sky, accompanied by flashes of lightning and boiling black clouds.

I tried to speak, but someone had sneaked into my throat and clogged it with sharp gravel. I cleared out the chat and squeaked, "I didn't put it there." Strictly speaking, that was true. But I was evading and she knew it.

"Child, do not lie to your grandmother!" she boomed, sounding like the Philadelphia Symphony playing doom music. "You do know how the deer came to be there, don't you?"

"I'm not lying," I stalled. I'd always believed that grandmothers were twinkly little old ladies who spoiled you rotten. Mine was the equivalent of the Bogie Man, except I wasn't as afraid of him.

"I didn't put him there," I said again. "He was after the tobacco." My mother stepped into the periphery of my vision.

"Mother, Bobby can't be responsible," she began.

"Be quiet!" my grandmother ordered, not even looking at my mother. "This child knows something. If he has done something wrong, he will be punished."

"I haven't done anything wrong!" I shouted, fed up with deer and tobacco and every other damn thing else. It seemed that everything I did was wrong. "Why don't you just get Uncle Al to shoot me too while he's shooting everything else? Then you wouldn't have to worry any more."

My grandmother's face turned dark, a mask of pure anger. That an insignificant pup like me should talk back to her was the height of insubordination. She raised a regal hand and pointed her lethal finger at me. "Child, you are going to get the worst whipping of your life!"

Suddenly my mother stepped between us. "Now, just a minute, Mother," she said, with steel in her usually mild voice. "I want to remind you that this is *my* son and if there is any disciplining to be done, his father and I will do it. You may be able to work your will on me, but you're not going to do it to my children. Is that clear?"

She and her mother stood locked in a struggle of will which, normally, my grandmother would have won hands-down. But my mother, her chick threatened, showed her heritage with an exhibition of inflexible will of her own. I saw a flicker of what appeared to be admiration. She looked at me. I pursed my lips to keep them from quivering and glared back at her. If my mom could stand up to the old grizzly, then so could I.

It was my grandmother who cracked first. "Albert, you'd better see to your truck," she ordered, turning to Uncle Al. "I think you killed it."

My mother wormed the entire story out of me. When I finished, she looked at me with something approaching awe, then with compassion. She shook her head and left the room.

Later that night, my mother and grandmother made up. "Mother," I heard my mother say, with suppressed laughter. "Why don't we have venison for supper?"

There was a long silence.

"Are you absolutely certain they didn't switch babies on you in that hospital?" my grandmother asked. But she didn't sound serious.

At least, I don't think she did.

JUST A LITTLE GAME OF SNOOKER

Kelly's Pool Parlor was owned by a man named Leibowicz, but Leibowicz was a realist and called it Kelly's because he knew there could be no place called Leibowicz's Pool Parlor.

Even in the days before pasteurized pool halls to which you could take your sainted mother, Kelly's was a clean place. Mr. Leibowicz insisted his chewing customers be accurate. Consistent missers of the spittoons were turned out with the warning not to return until they either quit chewing or passed a rigorous gunnery test.

Those whom he suspected of writing dirty doggerel on the restroom wall, he banished to the street with the admonition: "So you want to be an author, go home and sit in a closet and write dirty books!" My cousins, Hal and Frank, and I never had shot pool, but we ached to do so, mostly because we'd been told we shouldn't.

Our mothers and my grandmother had forbidden us to enter Kelly's under threat of death or worse. Worse was reform school where we knew muscular ladies with lank hair, hard faces, and gray dresses beat the whey out of little kids like us and sent us to bed without our suppers (or, even worse, with only creamed broccoli and bread for supper).

It was my grandmother whom we most feared, for she had the presence of an eagle, the majestic authority of a 15-star general. "The boy who shoots pool," she declared ringingly, looking rather pointedly at me, "could be delivering papers instead of lollygagging around."

I was sort of a n'er-do-well, just loafing around and sponging off my folks. I always figured 11 was too early to start earning a living, but my grandmother didn't. *Her* kids had been out selling home-baked bread as soon as they learned to make change. My grandmother was a Birch Lake pioneer; her children were as tough as whipcord. But her grandkids! Well, Frank and Hal and I quite obviously were incipient pool shooters and that wasn't just trouble in River City. That was trouble anywhere. The fact that she was right was immaterial.

August is the slack month in Birch Lake. It is the dog days. Birch Lake greens up with a rich growth of algae and fishing simply ceases. The tourists opt for the tavern where the beer is cool, even if the air isn't. It is too hot to do anything but lie around and pant, even if you are not a dog. A haze of dust hovers over the fields, which are dry and hot and tickle the nose. Tar melts and puddles on the roads, and beware! ye boy who gets into it and tracks tacky footprints home on hot tennis shoes!

Hal and Frank and I spent a lot of time lying up in the town ice house, that wondrous place of wet sawdust and cool, damp air. Many of the world's great problems, such as the potential source of admission money to the Durango Kid serial at the Rialto, the best place to dig earthworms (behind my grandmother's barn was a mammoth manure pile, a veritable Sutter's Creek lode of salubrious crawlers), and what had gone wrong with Bamburger's ice cream cones, were discussed here.

"I bet Jack Armstrong gets killed by the Dark Fiend," Frank said idly, hoping vaguely to start an argument.

"Dumbhead, they ain't gonna kill the hero," Hal sneered. Seldom did he call his little brother anything but dumbhead, but there was no real rancor in it.

"Okay," I asked, "how's he gonna get out of the snakepit

without the jaguar getting him?" I really didn't care. It would do the rest of that hapless bunch that hung around with the All-American Boy good to make do without him for a while.

"Who cares?" Hal said, echoing my thoughts. "I like Captain Midnight better anyway. My butt's getting wet." He brushed off the damp, clinging sawdust. "Let's go over to Kelly's and shoot a little game of snooker. What do you say?"

"Yeah. And let's go jump off the dam. You know Grandma would murder us and probably whip us, too."

"How's she gonna know?" Hal said. "She don't go to the pool hall."

"She'd know," I said darkly. My grandmother could see through walls and, not only that, she could dissolve them with an acetylene stare. I was convinced of it.

"You're as chicken as a yardful of turkeys," Hal sneered illogically. I always knew better than to rise to his challenges, for they invariably got me in deep trouble, but I never was able to resist.

"Oh, yeah!" I shouted. "I'll show you who's chicken!" And so we found ourselves in front of Kelly's Pool Parlor. We could see dim figures moving around inside. The window was time-stained. We huddled in the doorway like ducklings at their first mud puddle, figuring Mr. Leibowicz would drive us out, saying, "Shame! Little boys can't even see over the table shooting snooker! Go home to Annie-Over!"

But Mr. Leibowicz, who would have voted for a Gaboon viper had it been running on the Democratic ticket, was engaged in vilifying Herbert Hoover, Thomas Dewey, and the poor fishing in Birch Lake which he also blamed on the Republicans.

We skulked to the back and stood before our first pool table. A shaded light threw the table in stark relief to the rest of the ill-lit place. The cool green cloth was as a fresh forest to a desert-jaded old prospector. The white cue ball glistened and beckoned in a corner by itself, fairly quivering with latent kinetic energy. The tight-racked solids and stripes huddled defensively in triangular symmetry, daring us to destroy their massed authority.

We picked out cues. I sighted down mine, but I couldn't remember whether they were supposed to be straight or have a bend in them. It seemed logical that a good bend would enable a shooter to put a lot of english on the cue ball, so I chose one with a definite arc from butt to tip.

"Your break, Bobby," Hal ordered. Reluctantly, I sighted down the table. It looked as big as a football field. I had a terrible fear of ripping the cloth and owing Mr. Leibowicz all my allowance for the next two hundred years, so I turned the curved tip up to prevent it from diving into the table, laid the cue across my thumb and forefinger, and stroked hard.

The cue tip skipped off the top of the cue ball. My trailing hand slammed into the edge of the table and I dropped the cuestick which clattered endlessly on the concrete floor while I chased it and turned several hot shades of red.

"You kids watch the equipment back there, you hear!" shouted Mr. Leibowicz into the embarrassed silence at our end of the pool hall.

"Strike one!" Frank chortled. I could have killed him. I gritted my teeth, furrowed my brow, and tried again. The cue ball leaped from the cue tip, ricochetted off the right side cushion, caromed to the back end of the table, missed the racked balls entirely, hit the left side cushion, and sped across the table to thunk solidly into the corner pocket at my right hand.

"Good shot!" Hal exclaimed. I suggested he go peel a grape.

We waited for the cue ball to drop into the table tray, but it didn't. "Must be stuck," Hal said. I stuck my hand in the pocket and wriggled it around and felt the smooth surface of the ball with my fingertips.

"Here it is," I said. "I think I can get it." I reached farther back, trying to work my fingers around the ball so I could pull it out, but the slippery thing edged away from me. It was maddening. I strained my arm farther in the ball channel. The top of the table bit into my forearm and my elbow pressed painfully into the pocket cushion.

"There. I almost had it," I grunted. "Just a little more——uhhhh!" My arm slipped into the pocket. I had the ball.

Or more accurately, as I quickly discovered, the ball had me. My hand was closed around it, but when I tried to withdraw it, the bulk of the ball snugged my hand up against the ball channel and wedged it there. I didn't have enough room to let go of the ball and I couldn't pull it out. I was trapped.

Visions of Floyd Collins, the Titanic, and other disasters of entrapment flooded my mind and I was filled with numb terror. "I'm caught!" I croaked.

"Come on," Hal said. "Quit fooling around."

"I'm not fooling!" My voice quavered upward.

Hal had known me a long time and had seen me get into one improbable situation after another, so he looked at my quivering lips and tear-bright eyes and instantly believed me.

"Let's whittle off his arm," Frank suggested, giggling.

"It's not funny!" I trilled hotly. "I'm *caught!*"

"Well, we got to tell Mr. Leibowicz," Hal said.

"You can't! He'll tell Grandma!" I wailed.

"Well, you can't stay there till dark," Hal pointed out. "He'd notice you when he closed up. And your ma'd miss you maybe. He won't tell Grandma either. Everybody in Birch Lake knows her, and Mr. Leibowicz knows how much trouble she could make. He ain't gonna tell her."

Mr. Leibowicz was reluctant to let the Republicans off the ropes where he had them, but he came back and regarded me with a mixture of exasperation and amusement, his hands on his hips. "So you got yourself caught in my pool table," he said. "Well, we probably can get you out."

But he couldn't.

He tried pulling gently on my arm, but all that did was snug my hand tighter. He tried a harder pull which made me yelp. That scared him. "Don't yell, little boy!" he pleaded. "I'll get you out." He gnawed his knuckles, visions of a battalion of outraged parents with family attornies all waving summonses distracted him. Mr. Leibowicz was no fool. He knew how easy it is for snooker to become a cause celebré.

"We got to get Charley Hawkins," he said. Hawkins was the town carpenter. He sent one of the pool hall loafers to get Charley, and the loafer told every person he met on the way that some dumb kid had his arm caught in a pool table down to Kelly's. Birch Lake began to gather. Birch Lake entertainment was where you found it.

Charley looked at the problem from all angles, then announced the table would have to come apart. Mr. Leibowicz was not made happy by this news. Charley shrugged. "I can take the table apart or cut off the kid's arm. It's your choice."

I wailed in fright. "He's only kidding, little boy, only kidding!" Mr. Leibowicz told me hastily. "Okay, already, take the table apart. And do it quick. We got half of Wisconsin in here already. This kind of publicity I don't need."

I was afraid to look when Charley attacked the table with crowbar and chisel. There was the sound of wood splintering.

"Anybody else I charge a nickle a game," Mr. Leibowicz told me sourly. "For you, the price is two hundred dollars."

It wasn't easy to bite back the tears and a couple did get away and slide down my cheek. I was aware of the people crowding into Kelly's to see what a really stupid kid could do without half trying. "Geez, kid," Charley said, grunting over his labors. "What ever made you do such a dumb thing?"

I didn't answer. My lips trembled. The cue ball in my hand was slick with sweat. I would have liked to cram it in Hal's ear for ever suggesting a little game of snooker.

The steadily rising crescendo of wood rending, screws squeaking, and glue joints popping had Mr. Leibowicz wailing and moaning like a professional mourner.

Pool tables don't give up easily. By now, Kelly's was solidly packed with Birch Lakers. Hal and Frank stood white-faced at the edge of the crowd. Relief that it wasn't them was far more apparent in their attitudes than sympathy for a cousin and fellow kid in trouble.

What would my grandmother say? Or, what would she do? Stake me to an anthill? I considered it possible. Perhaps just lash me down firmly to the railroad tracks. My mother was malleable to a point. But Grandmother? She made chromium look like soft lead.

If only I'd ever done anything to make Grandma respect me. But the first time we ever visited her, she caught me eating dirt (I wanted to see why earthworms like it) and once I got her attacked by a buck deer and let a bear eat her Bluegill Festival cookie contest entry and I let that roadgrader get away and level half of Birch Lake. All the terrible, dumb things I'd ever done paraded before me, like a shambling platoon of misfits passing in review before an agonized commander.

Possibly Grandma would set me adrift on an ice flow then tell the polar bears where I was.

The crowd parted, like the Red Sea before Moses, and I looked a thousand miles in the air and there was my grandmother. She glared down at me. It was like being looked at by Thor, Wodin, and a few other guys known to tromp around in the clouds. Instinctively, I checked her hands to make sure she wasn't carrying any thunderbolts. Her expression could have cowed Zeus.

Charley gave a last grunt, the last glue joint collapsed, and my arm popped free. Darts of pain shot from my fingertips to the elbow and back again. I dropped the cue ball and it clicked sharply against the concrete floor, again and again, echoing in the hefty silence. Grandmother's lips sliced a dark, tight scar across her face, an ominous sign. The silence in Kelly's was the same as it is when a summer day turns suddenly dark and the birds fly low to the glassy water on the lake and you know there is a terrible storm nearing.

With awesome majesty, my grandmother turned to Mr. Leibowicz, who instinctively cowered. "What do you mean by enticing mere boys to this sin den!" she thundered at him. It was not a question. Mr. Leibowicz, however, was a man of character and he drew himself up proudly.

"You should have such a nice pool hall in your home!" he thundered back illogically. "Can I help it if you got kids who don't know from keeping their arms out of the machinery!"

For once my grandmother was somewhat nonplussed. For one thing, no one ever thundered back at her. She was defending an indefensible position——me. All she had on her side was might; right belonged to Mr. Leibowicz. She decided to retreat, making it look as nearly as possible like a resounding victory.

"Come with me," she ordered me imperiously and she whirled and marched for the door. I shambled in her wake, my arm red and swollen, my eyes the same. The crowd parted respectfully, honored to have been on the scene when a complete foulup displayed his dubious talents.

"Geez!" one guy whispered to his friend. "Look at that kid's *arm!*"

"Wait till you see his backside tonight," snickered the other man. I wished I were in Nepal, about nine-tenths of the way up an especially remote Himalaya. The crowd slowly broke up and my grandmother and I found ourselves halfway down the block by the bench in front of the Post Office.

She stopped, turned, and towered over me, a fierce pioneer figure in black silk, looking down on soft, decadent (and dumb) Youth. I knew how a pimply yardbird feels at a general court martial. No excuse, sir. Yes, sir, I'm dumb, dumb, dumb. Perry Mason wouldn't touch this case with a 10-foot subpoena. Tears drizzled down my cheeks and lodged in the corner of my mouth.

"Sit down," my grandmother commanded. I sat in numb, dumb

misery. I heard the rustle of Grandmotherly clothing. "Let's see your arm," she ordered. I held up my throbbing arm and she felt lightly over it. There was a long silence.

Here it comes, I thought. *Anthill or ice flow or Foreign Legion.*

I looked up at my grandmother, determined to take it like a man. There were a thousand wrinkles around her eyes, all turned up, like smiles. "I think," she said thoughtfully, "that what you need is a double-dipper ice cream cone."

This sank in slowly, like a rock tossed in quickmud, then it registered. In disbelief, I watched as a gentle smile broke across her face and the frosty blue eyes which had thunderstruck me on many an occasion softened and sparkled.

"Huh?" I gawped with quick intelligence.

"Two scoops——a double dipper. Chocolate on the bottom and vanilla on top."

Geez! She even knew to call it a double dipper. You just never can tell about grandmothers.

THE DAY THE DURANGO KID
GOT WHIPPED BY A LITTLE GIRL

If someone had told me that a girl of golden curls and fathomless blue eyes and complexion of rosebud and milk would become infatuated with me and follow me around with liquid gazes, I'd have been as appalled as if someone had told me that John Wayne was giving up western movies to become a hairdresser.

Birch Lake summers were for fishing and swimming and exploring and kick-the-can. Not for mooing and bawling like a lovesick calf. Why I entranced Jeannie surpassed reason. I was not exactly a twentieth century sex symbol. I sported the profile of a paper clip. I had snake hips and my ribs were countable from a block away. I preferred to think of myself as wiry, but everyone else said I was as skinny as a tomato stake.

Girls flustered me in general and Jeannie, from the moment we locked stares in Bamburger's Grocery Store, flustered me in particular. My blush threshold was subnormal. Talking with girls caused me to flame and sweat and drop such conversational gems as "Yeah, well, I guess."

I knew Jeannie only as a girl of unusual charm who lived on the other side of town, sat on the other side of the classroom, and was as unapproachable as someone on the other side of the moon.

Then, one stunning day at Bamburger's, where we bought ice cream cones, candy bars, and gumballs, she fell in love with me. My cousins, Hal and Frank, and I had wandered into Bamburger's one hot summer morning in search of a double dipper, chocolate on top, vanilla in the cone. Jeannie was standing by the soft drink cooler, a bottle of Seven-Up raised within three inches of her rosebud lips, when our eyes locked (the view was slightly obstructed by a strip of flypaper).

"My mom said she'd tan my fancy if she caught me lassoing the chickens anymore," Hal was saying. Hal was studying to be the Durango Kid.

"Let's go over to the ice house and cool off," Frank suggested. "I'm about to burn up. You comin', Bobby? Hey, Bobby? Bobby, you comin'?"

I was adrift in sweet confusion, staggered by a Cupidal dart as keen as a new Gillette Blue Blade. Jeannie's eyes were wide and astonished and her Seven-Up foamed and fizzed unheeded. Strengthless, we were unable to break the heavy stares which immobolized us. Had I not been with my cousins, I probably would have said hello and she would have said hello and we would have stumbled on into a jittery adolescent romance, replete with mushy notes and hand holding and other innocences. But I had to have my mouthy cousins with me.

Frank, unable to get my attention, followed my moo-cow stare to its destination, then looked back at me. He raised his eyebrows devilishly and jabbed Hal in the ribs. "What's the matter, Li'l Sweet Bobby?" he simpered sickeningly. "Got somethin' in your eye?"

I tumbled off the meteor I was riding and fell to earth. Jeannie exhaled, completed her swig of pop, and turned away, reddening. I remembered nothing from the past few moments. It was as if I had taken a dizzying trip around the moon, faster than light. I was weak all over.

Frank's buzzsaw voice nipped at me like a small, angry dog. "Bobby's got a girruullllll!" he keened, guffawing coarsely.

Heat pulsed in my face. "Have not!" I shouted, shoving him

against the gumball machine. "Let's go lasso the chickens!"

"You want my rope?" Hal sniggered. "Then you can go lasso that chicken." He and Frank leaned on each other and whooped.

"Ahhhh!" I snarled, searching for a biting retort and not finding one. "Go fly a monkey!" I meant to say, "Go fly a kite!" or "Go stuff a monkey!" but it came out all wrong. In that awful moment of embarrassment, I did a childish thing. I blamed Jeannie for it and thought I hated her. She had caused my embarrassment. Girls, for crying out loud, who needs them? Even as I scorned her, though, I remembered that melting look and I had a momentary feeling my chest was going to split like a ripe watermelon dropped on the ground.

After that, I avoided Jeannie as if she were threatening to beat me up, but she plagued me. I went down to the dam to swim and she came along and looked soulfully at me. "Hi, Bobby," she said shyly. "Are you swimming?"

"No," I growled, like Billygoat Gruff. "I'm folding parachutes." She mistook biting sarcasm for humor and giggled helplessly. I gritted my teeth. All right, so I despised her. Then why was I hiding in water up to my neck, ashamed for her to see my corduroy rib cage and chicken muscles? "Look, Jeannie," I pleaded, "why don't you go home? I think your mother is calling you." I watched the road, panicked lest Hal and Frank come along and whisper and giggle and point at me.

"I think I'll sit here and watch the water," Jeannie said, blistering me with a thousand-watt smile. "You be careful and don't go over the dam." I growled and dogpaddled down the shore without looking back. When I put my feet down, she was right above me on the bank.

"You sure do dogpaddle good," she said admiringly.

"So do dogs," I answered shortly. She giggled.

Horror of horrors, Jeannie's mother and mine became co-chairmen of the annual Birch Lake Pie Supper. They were as close as sisters while they planned the event, and suddenly Jeannie was at our house incessantly, mooning around me and asking if I liked to read Nancy Drew mysteries. It was terrible.

On the second Saturday before the Pie Supper, Hal and Frank and I followed our normal schedule. We attended the matinee at the Birch Lake Rialto, a tin-sided movie theater which offered a dirty screen, plush splintered plywood seats, and the thick atmosphere of an old locker room. But it showed and had been showing for a long time the continuing western adventures of the Durango Kid. In Chapter 50, we had left our hero hanging from a cliff by one bleeding hand. A sinister character called Black Bart was stomping viciously on the Kid's clutching fingers. The Kid stared somewhat apprehensively into the yawning abyss and tried to ignore Black Bart's grinding boot. But it was no go, and he fell free and began to plunge to certain death. The scene froze and the music came up dramatically.

"Will this mean the end of the Durango Kid?" asked the off-screen narrator.

"*No!*" we shouted in unison and whistled and stomped.

"And what of Brave Feather, the proud Indian companion of the Kid, now staked to an anthill in the desert?" our noisy interrogator asked.

"*Let the ants eat him!*" we screamed.

"Be sure to be here next week for Chapter 51, the Pit of Death!" cried the voice. There was a vast clacking of rickety seats. We crunched through a summer's accumulation of popcorn fallout and squinted into the bright sun.

"Golly!" Hal exclaimed. "How do you suppose they're gonna get him out of that mess-up?"

"They'll probably have Brave Feather's people in a cave somewheres down in that pit," Frank mused thoughtfully, for he was a student of movie serial technique. "You know, they'll be standing there when he comes flyin' by, and the best lassoing Indian will throw a rope over him and they'll drag him into their secret hideaway where they got skulls of their enemies and torches and all that good junk."

And that is precisely what happened in Chapter 51, which ran the week before the Pie Supper.

We were riding an emotional high when the serial episode ended and were suddenly stunned when our off-screen confidant announced, "Be sure to be here next week for the final installment of 'The Perilous Adventures of the Durango Kid!' Will the Kid escape the dreadful spring gun which Black Bart has fiendishly set in the anthill where Brave Feather is staked? See the savage uprising by Brave Feather's people. Will the President, riding the train from Abilene to Wichita, fall into Black Bart's trap and be kidnapped? And how can the Kid possibly survive the fall between the hurtling boxcars?"

"Whew!" Frank breathed awestruck. "I can't figure *no* way out of that can of worms!" The final episode was the entertainment highlight of the summer for every kid in Birch Lake. Every kid in town was going to be there, come high water or chicken pox. Everyone, it turned out, but me. On Thursday, my mother stunned me by announcing firmly that *my* Saturday afternoon would be spent helping her work on the Pie Supper. No amount of whining would change her mind. The Pie Supper chores were the worst possible fate and I just knew old dumb Jeannie was behind the whole thing. Probably spend all afternoon reading me selected passages from Nancy Drew. I concentrated on hating Jeannie of the dumb bouncy curls and big old eyes.

Seething, I stalked toward town, kicking rocks. The last people I wanted to see were Hal and Frank, but naturally I met them. "Hey, Bobby," Frank said, "you got any ideas on how the Durango Kid is gonna wind everything up?"

"I'm not going," I muttered. "I gotta help on the pie thing." They registered sympathy, and then a slow smile slithered over Frank's face, like an ugly snake. "Hey! I'll bet you're gonna take Little Miss Dolly Curls to the great big Pie Supper. Bobby's got a girruuulllll!"

I growled and shoved him and he stumbled back and fell over his mother's prize peace rose and howled in pain. "You leave my brother alone!" Hal cried, jumping on me. We crashed to the ground, scuffling and shouting inarticulate hate slogans.

Their mother broke it up and I stalked on downtown, brooding on man's inhumanity to man. Score another one for Jeannie. If I'd had a dog, she'd have figured out a way to make him bite me.

"Hi, Bobby." The shy, soft voice made me jump and I whirled to face dumb old Jeannie. She stood there with that melting, tender look on her big-eyed face. Don't tell me she didn't know how cute she was! For a moment I forgot how much I hated her. "My mother said you might go to the Pie Supper," she murmured shyly. Boy, that did it! The mention of the Pie Supper detonated me.

"Why don't you leave me alone, you dopey dope!" I shouted. "I'm not gonna go to any Pie Supper with you! I wouldn't take you to a dog show if I thought you'd win first prize! Why don't you go crawl in a hole and pull it in after you! Leave me alone!"

There was a terrible silent moment after I ran out of dreadful things to say, during which she merely looked starkly at me, her face gone white. "I thought," she whispered, "you liked me a little."

I felt my heart sliced with rusty hack saws. I bit my lip and looked at the ground and wished I could sink into a muskrat hole with the rest of the rats. I tried to say "I'm sorry," but my pride had a firm grip on my tongue and I couldn't get the words out. She turned and ran toward town, her shining curls flying in the sunlight.

Then my mother relented and said she wouldn't need me at the Pie Supper, and so it all was unnecessary. Saturday morning sparkled with the magic of summer and the day glittered with glory. Breakfast tasted like wet sawdust.

Hal and Frank and I stood around and dug our toes in the dirt and finally decided to make up. Everything was okay again. Then why did I feel as if someone were digging postholes in my heart?

The theater filled fast. This was the big one. I picked out a seat that seemed to be relatively free of old wads of gum. About now, I thought, my mother and Jeannie's mother and Jeannie would be gathering across the street at the Town Hall before the Pie Supper.

The house lights went out to a tumultuous cheer from the assembled youngsters. There flickered before our eyes the blurry title: "Chapter 52—The Last Desperate Moment!" A piece of lint lodged on the projector lens and vibrated there.

"Hey, Projector Man, get her mustache outta the machine!" cried a wit somewhere on the other side of the theater and everyone whistled and stomped. The lint flicked away and the Durango Kid swirled to a plunging halt. The scene changed to show Brave Feather staked to an anthill. I began to itch. About now, Jeannie would be unloading the pies and stuff across the street. Were her eyes still stricken, her cheeks white? I bit my lip.

"Brave Feather!" the Kid cried, sliding gracefully off his stallion to help his fallen companion.

"Hey, watch the spring gun, ya dumb bunny!" all the kids shouted. Then the great white stallion was there, whinnying and shoving the Kid away, pawing until he tripped the deadly spring gun harmlessly.

The two heroes galloped recklessly across a railroad trestle, intent on saving the President. This was it—Hal and Frank were transfixed, their eyes big. Big eyes. White, shocked face. "I thought you liked me a little."

"I gotta go!" I cried, leaping up. I shoved Frank out of the way. "What a dumb time to go to the bathroom!" he shouted.

I shoved and pushed my way to the aisle, ignoring the shouted insults of the boys whose view I blocked, and stumbled up the aisle, wading through the rifted popcorn and empty cups. I ran across the street, scooted up the steps and through the door of the Town Hall.

The room was filled with women—plump ones, skinny ones, tall ones, short ones. Jeannie was on the fringe of this matronly forest, her back to me. She turned and her big eyes widened.

"I *would* take you to a dog show!" I blurted. "I mean, I'm sorry about everything and I didn't mean what I said and—and—would you go to the Pie Supper with me?"

I ran out of breath and courage and gulped and felt like running. She smiled tremulously and diamonds came into her eyes and she said, "I'd like to go with you."

For all I know, the Durango Kid and Brave Feather both fell off the train and got trampled by the great white stallion, and Black Bart kidnapped the President and lived happily ever after. I really didn't care.

BEAR WITH ME

My Uncle Al thought it was the best Birch Lake benefit street dance and pie bazaar the town ever had, but nearly everyone disagreed with him, all the way from the mayor who was laid up for a week with a case of nervous hives that made him look like a relief map of Nepal to my father who only quit whipping me when his hand became sore.

Uncle Al might not have been as entertained if I had spotted him in the crowd. He was the family wildlife expert. He would not have laughed quite so heartily had I handed him my 500-pound problem.

The BLBSD & PB always came in deep summer when there wasn't much to do except laugh at the strange fishing lures the tourists bought, thinking they were going to catch big fish. The BLB etc. broke summer's lethargy. It was a day of festive abandon; however, my cousins, Hal and Frank, and I had let our abandon get out of hand the preceding year and that's why my father started off the day of the BLB etc. with a wry little lecture on responsibility and, above all, staying out of trouble.

His lectures were wry and entertaining when he was discussing the *possibility* of my getting into trouble, but when I'd gone and done it, the lecture turned severe and his whipping hand moved faster than his tongue.

"As you are well aware," he told me, "your conduct is not always exemplary. That means good," he added as I started to interrupt. "The fireworks display you conceived last year was not appreciated, especially the rocket that got away from you and pursued Mrs. Flakey across the Town Hall where she tripped and sat heavily in Mrs. Johnson's cherished first-place-winning banana cream pie."

I snickered.

"It's not funny!" my father said sharply. And of course it wasn't. Mrs. Flakey was a stylish stout and not built for joking. Hal and Frank and I never meant to do all those things. It was just that something always seemed to get away from us, like that dumb rocket that started out in a vacant lot and went through the Town Hall window. Or the time the road grader got away from me and knocked down half of Birch Lake. Or the time Hal and Frank and I got crossways with Elmer Blosser and he amost shot Old Lady Gunnison. Or the time——well, this year would be different. No trouble. Hal and I were going fishing. Frank was laid up with chicken pox, sweating, itching, and whining.

By July the streams were low and tea-colored, trout finned idly under logs and rocks, hoping for a harsh storm to churn needed oxygen into the sluggish water. The lakes were weedy and pea-soupy with algae. The blacktop roads smelled of tar and the ditches and fields creaked with the ardent stridulation of dusty insects. Tall flowers nodded and drowsed under the fierce sun, a sun that dominated a washed-out sky.

Hal and I headed for a pool on Thirty-Three Creek which we knew concentrated nice brook trout every summer. A patient boy could lie on his belly on the green creekside moss and ease a worm-baited hook into the water and shortly be playing a wriggling brookie. "Your dad talk to you about staying out of trouble?" Hal asked as we slipped into the woods. I nodded.

"Man, I never will forget all that hollerin' when that rocket went through the window!" Hal shook his head. He rubbed his rear end reflectively.

Thirty-Three Creek was jumpable in most place. It burbled over slick granite rocks, curling and chuckling through the woods, much of the time coyly hiding itself under an umbrella of matted alders. We found our pool, scoured from the pasty land by clear, icy spring water that tumbled over a foot-high ledge.

I lay on my belly on the spongy, cool-moist moss of the stream bank and threaded a dirt-crumbed worm on a tiny hook. Beneath me was an undercut bank where the bigger, warier brook trout lay, cool and protected, waiting for choice food morsels to eddy within range. I eased the worm into the water and got ready to jerk my antique split bamboo fly rod the instant something grabbed the bait.

The rod tip jerked down and the fish wriggled hysterically. I lifted him out, a 12-incher. Not bad.

And then I saw the bear cub just across the pool from me. "Rats!" Hal exclaimed as he lost a fish. I poked him. "Hey, watch it, big shot!" he growled. "Watch whose ribs you got your crummy elbows stuck in!" I hissed at him and pointed at the bear cub who, mildly alarmed, had scrambled head-high in a tiny tree that swayed with its weight. "Jeezle!" Hal breathed. "A *bear!*"

We splashed across the creek, trout stealth forgotten, and stood a respectful distance from the cub which peered over its shoulder at us.

As we stood with our mouth open, an idea sprouted in my mind and grew with the terrible ferocity of crabgrass. My inspirations always were so overpowering that they blinded me to any potential drawbacks. "You remember the year Clevis Clumber had that pet raccoon that danced to the mouth harp?" I asked. Hal nodded, frowning. He musta made a fortune with everybody throwing money. You know how them tourists get with some beer in them. I bet we could clean up with a bear."

"We can't play no mouth harp," Hal said, ever the logician.

"Man, when you got a *bear*, you don't *need* no dumb harmonica!" I exclaimed.

"We couldn't get him back to town," Hal said dubiously. "He's got teeth and stuff." I considered that problem and, unfortunately, ingenuity triumphed.

"My dad's backpack!" I barked. "My dad's got his thing with a big old bag that this old bear cub would stuff in like sausage in a gut!"

"I don't know," Hal muttered hesitantly.

"You keep this old bear up that tree and I'll get the pack!" I enthused, afire with the potential of bear ownership. I set off for home, a 15-minute run, found the pack, and was back in less than an hour.

Hal and the cub were staring at each other like two mistrustful dogs. "I don't think we oughta do this," Hal said doubtfully.

"What's the matter? You chicken?" I sneered.

"Them things got teeth!" he exclaimed.

"Well, so have you," I replied illogically. "But that don't mean you're gonna bite someone."

I approached the frightened bear cub. "Come on, little guy," I soothed. "Let's go for a ride." The animal calmed at my gentle voice. A regular St. Francis of Birch Lake, that was me. I carefully pried the cub loose from the tree and we stuffed him in the backpack like a hairy sleeping bag. He nestled there uneasily, blatting occasionally. We started toward town.

"Uncle Al's sure gonna be proud of us," I predicted. "He knows everything about the outdoors, and I bet he never brought a bear home."

"Maybe he's just got better sense," Hal replied, with rare perspicacity.

The roar behind me was so indescribably fearsome that it made every hair on my body spring to attention. It was a blast of undiluted rage. Hal and I whirled to see, not 20 paces away, a towering sow bear looming over us. Her lips were wrinkled back, disclosing wicked fangs that looked as big as piano keys. Her little eyes were blood red and her fur was rigid with fury. The bear cub bleated and the she-bear snarled, a savage rumble that melted my bones. She swatted aside a sizeable sapling as if it were a seedling tomato plant and it was obvious even to an idiot such as I that she was about to charge.

Hal and I did what we invariably did in situations of crisis. We ran like hell.

No kid handicapped by a 25-pound bear cub can outrun an enraged she-bear, but we gained a bit of respite when the mama, maddened by her anger, tripped over a log and fell into a vine-choked gully. By the time she ripped apart the clinging greenery and got herself sorted out, we were out of sight and picking up speed. She had to use her hearing, rather than sight, and it slowed her down momentarily.

I tried to drop the pack, but the belt buckle jammed. I tore at it as I ran, but the effort was awkward and slowed me. Then the she-bear gallop out of the woods, her big head high, wind scenting my red-hot trail. I raced down the tracks, wishing devoutly for a

Unencumbered by the bear, Hal made better time and flitted out of sight. No Olympic sprinter could have caught him, and few if any world class runners ever had had the same incentive. I reached the edge of the woods and scrambled up the high railroad bank, slipping in the loose cinders. The outskirts of town were a hundred yards ahead.

I paused to gulp a ragged breath but immediately saw the she-bear gallop out of the woods, her big head high, wind scenting my red-hot trail. I raced down the tracks, wishing devoutly for a passenger train to come along and pick me up and take me to anywhere else.

My terror-clabbered mind was aswirl with survival plans. Perhaps Uncle Al could deal with an enraged bear——hypnotize it or something. I had great, if misplaced, faith in Uncle Al. Perhaps my grandmother could skin it with one of her Bowie-blade glares.

Main Street was jammed with people, roped off for the annual day-long concert and dance. A country-and-western group was in the throes of "Born To Lose," an appropriate selection as it turned out, and electric guitars throbbed with bucolic heartache.

I rounded the corner by the hardware store and plunged toward an opening in the mob. A woman screamed, "A bear! A bear!" If she could see it, the she-bear was far too close. I picked up speed and the crowd parted as the Red Sea must have fallen before Moses. I sped through the corridor of stampeding people with far less confidence than Mr. Moses and saw the stage directly ahead of me.

I sprinted up the steps as the band went over the back side, leaving in mid-air an assemblage of amplified instruments which clattered to the stage floor with the loudest electronic crescendo in musical history. The she-bear was so close that I heard her teeth popping together with the explosive sound of a mammoth mouse trap. And I was the mouse.

At the top step I made one frenzied final effort to loosen the jammed belt buckle and it finally popped free. I squirted out of the pack, dived through the drummer's vacated station, and slid off the back side of the stage to the street. I scrambled to my feet, staggered to the sidewalk, and collapsed in front of Bamburger's Grocery. I was done. If she wanted me, she could have me.

The bear cub crept out of the pack. His mother sniffed him, checking for damage. Finding none, she swung her head, growling, peering with eyes of fire for something to blame. I shrank against the storefront, trying to look like an inoffensive gumball machine.

The bear studied the fallen musical instruments, then scooped up a guitar as if it were a rotten log filled with juicy grubs. The speakers wailed mournfully and she snarled and flung the guitar to the street. It crashed with a discord that sounded like Bob Wills accompanying a tank battle. The sound enraged the bear and she began to dismember musical instruments right and left. The noise was deafening. There were bass runs and progressive chords that would have sent Duke Ellington back to basics.

Finally it was too much for the overloaded amplifiers and they shorted out with a blinding flash of unchanneled energy and a cloud of acrid white smoke. Electricity surged through the bear and knocked her ten feet across the stage and over the edge, where she lay dazed in the wreckage she had caused. The cub crept down the steps, bleating anxiously.

The she-bear struggled to her feet, shaking her head, all her aggression drained by that brief exposure to electrotherapy. The two bears trotted toward the edge of town and presently vanished around a corner.

Everyone agreed it was the most unusual street dance ever held in Birch Lake. The country band, sobered by the demonstrated potential of electricity, took their insurance money and bought nonamplified folk instruments and became a bluegrass band.

I spent a lot of time skulking around Birch Lake to avoid being pointed out to tourists as "the kid that started it all."

The only positive result I could see was that the track coach, who had been in the crowd, urged me to be sure and go out for distance running.

"WE DIDN'T DO NOTHING, MOM"

My Uncle Al liked to hunt and fish almost as well as he liked to drink. Between his outdoor activities and his drinking, he managed to fill his waking hours with many happy moments.

When the sun dappled the blue waters and the air was soft and warm, Uncle Al appeared at the Birch Lake dam, fishing rod and baitbox in hand. He scrambled down the steep bank on the Birch River side of the dam to his old wooden canoe, which he kept tied to a stout alder.

Some mornings, however, after he had been attacked by a virulent hop at my Uncle Floyd's tavern, he was unable to report for duty. It was just such a morning that I lost his canoe and my cousin Hal.

Hal and I were engaged in aimless time killing near the canoe mooring. The old canoe was scarred and weathered. Gouges in the green sides were testimony to its having hit more than one rock during a busy life.

Uncle Al took the canoe, which he called the "Birch River Bitch" (sometimes affectionately; more often not) down the rock-strewn, twisting, swift river for a dozen miles with experienced ease. Hal and I never had been in a canoe in our lives and wouldn't have known its stern from our own.

Uncle Al started his floats below the dam and went to the County Highway E bridge, which spanned the beginning of the wildest, most dangerous rapids in Wisconsin. Even Uncle Al wouldn't challenge that froth which, if its preliminaries didn't get you, culminated in a frenzied 12-foot waterfall that would eat a canoe and occupants like a junkyard hound eats a cupcake.

Hal and I were flipping rocks into the river that morning, watching them skip, idly making million-dollar bets on who could get the most skips. "Boy," Hal said, apropos of nothing, "you sure get in more trouble than any kid I ever knew."

Perhaps he was talking about the time I got my arm caught in the pool table at Kelly's or the time I rode a runaway road grader down the main street of Birch Lake. There were some other things, too.

"Well, you're not so perfect either," I riposted with devastating wit (though he nearly was —— he never got caught). I shied a flat rock which sank with a thick *chunk*! "I don't try to mess up."

"I'd hate to be around if you ever start trying," Hal said. He got up, shimmied as he brushed clinging sand from his britches, and wandered over to Uncle Al's canoe, which lay heeled over slightly, its prow (or stern, for all I knew) bobbing in the eddy. There was some rainwater collected in one end of the canoe. Hal stepped in and picked up a rusty old coffee can. He started bailing. I stretched luxuriously on shore. Water roared over the dam upstream, but its angry crashing was muted to a gentle whisper down where we were, a soothing aquatic lullaby. I breathed deeply of the fragrant, clean, summery air. Yes, sir, it was going to be a good day, all right!

This euphoria lasted all of two minutes.

Hal moved in the canoe, causing the landbound end to grate on the gravel. Filled with concern for Uncle Al's treasured old Bitch, only trying to help, I thought moving it might be beneficial. It was when I was serving mankind that things generally went to hell.

I bent over and grabbed the canoe and heaved it toward a more comfortable position. I couldn't move the heavy canoe much, but it was enough to throw Hal off balance. He was kneeling on the thwart. He slipped and fell face forward over the stern seat. The prow rose sharply and slipped from my grasp.

The quick current grabbed the canoe, jerked it off shore and into the river as Hal came up sputtering. I stood stunned. The thing was supposed to be tied!

"Darn you!" Hal cried, anger reddening his face. "What the heck are you doing!" At first he didn't wonder that he was now 20 feet away from me with the gap steadily widening. The tie rope, wrapped around a broken willow sprout, floated out behind the canoe.

Finally, stung to activity, I splashed into the stream, but a vagrant current dipped the rope under my reaching fingers, then it was gone into the deep water. The eddying current tugged at my legs like mean little kids, trying to knock me down.

Hal suddenly realized he was adrift, literally up a creek without a paddle and headed down it at a terrifying speed. His eyes grew big and round. "Help me!" he quavered. The canoe hit a rock and he clutched the gunwales in fright. The big craft rocked, bounced around the boulder, and surged on downstream.

"What can I do?" I shouted, hoping he had some good ideas in mind. He didn't. There was nothing either of us could do. The river was solidly lined for miles with dense alders. Part of it was through a deep, inaccesible gorge, part through a remote and treacherous bog. Once in the river, you stayed in it until you came to a crossing. And that first crossing was the Highway E bridge at the mouth of the killer rapids.

Hal was about to vanish around the first bend. I raised my hand and waved goodbye. It seemed an insufficient gesture, but it was all I could think of. He gave me a forlorn little wave in reply. He looked small and wretched, not 10 feet tall, the way he looked when he was beating me up.

All sorts of terrible thoughts raced through my head, led by one churlish scold that warned, "You're gonna get it for getting your shoes wet!"

How could I tell Hal's mother what had happened? "Now, Aunt Ruth, don't get excited, but Hal is going down the river without a paddle." No, that sounded like some kind of joke.

How about "Could we take a ride down to the Highway E bridge and see if Hal is there yet?" That way, I could ease gently into the problem. But telling anyone what had happened appealed to me about as much as trading places with Hal would have and I wanted to explore every possible solution before I did that. I ran up the hill toward the dam, hoping for inspiration.

As if I didn't already have enough problems, I saw Uncle Al ambling down the street near the bar. He didn't look like much more than my shaggy old uncle, but he was a man deeply gripped by decision. Should he get a can of Grandma's manure pile earthworms and go fishing, or should he stop by my Uncle Floyd's bar for a cool one. Oh, my gosh! If he decided to go fishing and found his canoe gone!

"Hi, Uncle Al!" I cried, running up to him. "Going in for a beer?" He pondered it, all whiskers and yellowy eyeballs. He had forgotten to put in his false teeth and the lack of ivory gave his face a sort of collapsed look, like a deflated football.

"Huh?" he asked, not very alertly. It was early.

"I mean," I babbled, fumbling for some way to deflect him from the river. "It sure is a hot day, isn't it? Makes a man really thirsty."

"Yeah," he mused. 'Yeah!" His faded eyes lit and he gaped a smile of gratitude at me for having given his day some direction. He turned in at the bar. Whew!

My thinking spot in Birch Lake was the town ice house, so I ran across the street and through a weedy pasture to it. The ice house was where we hid when things (such as the weather and our parents' temper) got too hot for comfort. I clambered to the loft and squatted in the cool air, my thoughts tangled. I chipped a piece of ice to help me think. I brushed the sawdust off and retired to the up-stairs window to mull. I sucked the ice and thought dreadful thoughts. Dragging the river for my cousin's body. My aunt's scream when they told her the news. My grandmother looming over me like an Alpine avalanche. I gnawed the ice in wild alarm. Do something, my father always told me. Even if it's wrong.

And then I chanced to glance down in the pasture behind the ice house and saw possible salvation in the form of a horse.

It wasn't much of a horse, but it was a chance. He belonged to a family I knew was out of town and his name was Blackie. He and I were fairly good friends. I fed him and he refrained from kicking or biting me. There was a set of buggy harness in his shed and the buggy itself, a topless, spring-seated old relic, sagged tiredly against the shed.

It was a threadbare chance, but it was better than what I

could expect if I went to Aunt Ruth and told her that one of her cubs even at that moment might be spinning in the frothing vortex of a savage whirlpool like a gerbil caught in a washing machine. I shuddered.

Blackie was unenthusiastic. "Hold still, you crummy old horse!" I shouted at him as he tried to back away from me. I held him by the halter and he dragged me halfway across the pasture before I could get him stopped.

"Now you listen to me, dumbhead!" I yelled, shaking my fist in his astonished face. "I got no time to be messing around with you! You just act right!" My frenzy must have convinced him he was beset by a madman and it would be best to act calm and hope I settled down. He stood resignedly the rest of the time I was throwing harness all over him and trying to figure out what went where and what hooked to what.

Finally I had the harness more or less connected. Blackie looked somewhat as if he had run into a leather spider web, but he was able to pull. Then I had to hitch on the buggy. First I tried pulling the buggy to the horse, but it was too heavy. I had to back the horse to the buggy and that was sheer hell. I wheezed raggedly with effort, knowing that every moment I wasted meant another few yards downstream for Hal. If I didn't get to Highway E before Hal did, he'd be sucked into the rapids and over the falls and be killed.

The dumb horse kept stepping on the loose straps and on me and skittering around.

Finally I got him hitched. I threw a coil of rope into the buggy and glanced feverishly around the shed for a life preserver, though of course I didn't find one. Just like a horse owner not to have a life vest. You never know when a horse is going to throw you in a lake.

"Giddyup, Blackie!" I shouted. And we were off.

My only advantage was that the river bent in a wide loop and the road ran straight. It was about a dozen miles to the bridge by water and only seven by road. But I couldn't convince Blackie there was any need for haste. "Move, you damn horse!" I shouted, hitting at him with the end of the rope. He flinched and shied but refused to break from a lurching jog which wasn't much faster than a walk.

"Come on, Blackie, be a good horse," I pleaded. It embarassed me to beseech a horse. It also didn't work. Blackie's ears leaned backward, so I knew he was listening to me, but he was adamant in his placid pace.

I continued to think terrifying thoughts. If I didn't save Hal and the canoe, they'd send me to reform school. Or everyone would pretend I didn't exist. Or they'd shut me up in the woodshed with my grandmother (who could ignite kindling merely by looking at it).

"Get up Blackie, you crummy old horse!" I whinnied in panic. The buggy creaked and jounced endlessly along the gravel road. We crept past farmhouses where cows ate sedately of the peaceful green grass and people worked and laughed and lived without care. How I envied them! The reins were slippery with the sweat of my fear.

A sign appeared ahead. The Highway E junction! I cracked Blackie a couple of times with the rope and he snorted in irritation. The road to the river slanted sharply downhill through scrub birch trees. Long before we got to the bridge, I heard the roar of the rapids, locally known as Tucker's Goodbye. Somewhere back in history, a man named Tucker had made the mistake of letting his boat get caught in the tumbling water. The river made matchwood out of the boat and a statistic out of him. The hundred-yard froth was named in his honor, a painful route to immortality.

I slowed Blackie to a halt and vaulted down to the dusty road, breathing quickly and shallowly with trembly fear. I ran out on the bridge and looked upstream to the first bend, but saw nothing.

Oh God! Suppose Hal already had swept under the bridge and into the rapids and even now was consanguineous chop suey!

I spun to look downstream and vertigo hit me with the force of a baseball bat. The bouncing, flying water seethed and twisted and smashed over and against the snaggly, jutting rocks so swiftly that it disoriented me. I staggered dizzily and nearly fell on the old wooden flooring of the bridge.

Just under where I stood, the water, smoothly gathering speed, was jerked sharply into the snarling rocks as if some giant hand had reached out angrily to gather in the water. Downstream was the falls, a sheer drop at whose bottom the water boiled in a seething, deadly backwave. Anything that went into it tossed and tumbled repeatedly before it finally spat out, torn and shredded into the rest of the rapids.

High-standing waves swayed like cobras across the river, and the water roared with the insensate fury of a pack of frenzied mandrills. Absolutely no one tried to run Tucker's Goodbye, as a well-worn portage path upstream testified. No one except maybe Hal.

My mouth quivered and turned down and I felt tears start.

For all I knew even now Hal was dead and the canoe a bunch of toothpicks somewhere downstream. I bit my lip and tried not thinking like that. I ran back to the buggy and got the rope.

If I dropped the rope off the bridge, maybe I could——no, that wouldn't work. Hal would be in the rapids before I took up the slack.

I started tearing Blackie loose from the buggy. "Now, listen, Blackie," I told him earnestly as I tore fingernails and raised welts on my arms. "This isn't any joke. You got to help out or else. Don't mess around. I'll buy you a bale of hay if you do it right. Okay?" I was glad there was no one around to see me cajoling a horse. It looked dumb and I'd already done enough dumb things for a brigade of boneheaded kids.

I pulled Blackie· down the portage path to where the river eddy slapped against the red sand bank. I threw the rope around his sweaty neck and tied some sort of knot in it——several hapless years as a Boy Scout hadn't done a thing for my knotability.

No sooner had I jerked the knot tight than I saw the canoe sweep around the bend fifty yards upstream, surging and bucking like a buffalo in a stampede. The craft skidded and slewed in the water, banged broadside into a rock, straightened out, and headed like an arrow down the middle of the river. Hal knelt in the back, trying to crush the aft thwart to sawdust with his fingers. His eyes looked like steak platters. He knew what was ahead. He considered jumping for it, but couldn't swim well enough to beat the current.

His only hope was for me to throw the rope to him. If I missed, he was gone. That was a simple and terrifying certainty. I splashed out in the stream as far as I dared, feeling the water chop at my legs. Blackie, bless him, stood firm on the bank.

"Hal!" I screamed, my voice nearly lost in the thunder of the rapids. "Over here!"

He saw me and hope lighted his face. I held up the rope and shook it. He nodded, the hope replaced by dire misgiving. He knew my accuracy with a baseball.

Now he was fifteen yards away. I didn't dare think or aim. I slung the rope with all my strength, praying it wouldn't foul or fall off-target.

Just as I threw it, the canoe struck its nose into an eddy and the stern, caught by the swift main current, started to swing broadside. The rope fell just an inch in front of the swinging canoe.

I cried out in despair. Hal scrambled over the thwart and

threw himself half out of the canoe, trying to reach the rope, but it bobbed just beyond his grasp. His expression turned sick with fright.

Just when I was sure he was lost, the rope snagged for an instant on a projecting rock and Hal made a last desperate lunge and caught it. He hauled it into the canoe and fell sprawling and the craft teetered and grated over the rock.

"Tie it to the canoe!" I shouted. Hal threw a quick loop around the bow thwart. The slack went out of the rope so quickly the water hissed. Hal got another loop around the thwart before the rope came taut, almost jerking poor Blackie into the river. The horse snorted and whinnied in distress and set his hooves into the sandy bank.

The rope thrummed like a guitar string. The canoe spun around into the eddy by the shore and banged hard into the willows, nearly turning over. It bobbed there for quite a while as Hal adjusted to the idea of still being alive. Finally he stumbled overboard into the shallow water and waded ashen-faced to me.

We sat together on the shore, our feet in the water, so tired we couldn't talk. Blackie nickered, rousing me.

"We got to get Blackie and the canoe home," I said. Hal looked blankly at me. He hadn't quite cleared the river out of his head. I pointed at Blackie. "I borrowed him," I said. "If we get him and the canoe home without anyone seeing us, no one will ever know about it. Unless you tell."

Hal brightened visibly, like dawn. "I don't think my mom would like to know about this," he said in a voice of measured reason. "She gets a headache from worrying about me crossing the street.

We had to devise a way to get the canoe back to Birch Lake. We considered (and rejected) throwing the canoe over Blackie's back, wading him upstream towing it, and dragging it along the highway behind him.

"We can get the front of it up on the buggy," Hal said. "But the hind end is gonna drag." Unless. I remembered passing a little house about a mile from the river. In front there was a mailbox supported by an old set of wagon wheels. I couldn't remember if anyone had been home.

Faithful old Blackie made the trip in fifteen minutes. We didn't shilly-shally. Together, grunting with the strain, we tipped the heavy set of wheels over. They nearly were rusted to the axle, but we trooped tiredly to the barn, then to a shed, finally unearthed a bucket of black, dripping grease.

It helped some. The wheels turned with shrieks and screams, as if someone were hitting a bunch of old ladies with a bullwhip. We towed the wheels slowly behind us back to the river. They tried persistently to run off the road, but I sat balanced precariously with my feet braced on the axle while Hal drove. Everything on me ached. I think I had total sprain.

It took us an hour to drag the canoe out of the river and up the steep bank, even with Blackie's patient help. Then we hoisted the front end of the canoe up on the wagon seat. We managed to lift, shove and scoot an inch at a time until the wheels (with the mailbox still attached) were underneath the stern. We lashed them more or less in line with the buggy wheels.

"We'll just have to let Blackie go real slow on his own," I said. "We can hold the canoe on the buggy."

Blackie sensed we finally were ready to head him back toward his beautiful, peaceful, pleasant, quiet pasture and he was more than willing to help. But it took some straining to get under way. Twice we stopped for minor adjustments to our jerryrig. Henry Ford's prototype wasn't all that perfect either.

The wheels screamed like shot rabbits, but they turned. Hal and I clung grimly to the canoe prow as it threatened to jerk loose from the buggy. Blackie drove himself. I was so tired I was punchy and didn't even hear the old Swedish farmer's car go off in the ditch in front of us.

He came around a bend and, so bemused was he by the sight of an apparently driverless horse and buggy all wrapped up to a wheeled canoe with a mailbox spinning on one side that he ran into the ditch and stopped. He immediately jumped out and grabbed Blackie by the halter. "Py doggies!" he shouted at us, shaking his fist, "what you tink dis is, eh, some kinda nuthouse!" He wouldn't let us go on until we unhitched poor old Blackie once again and helped haul his rusty old car out of the ditch. Grumpily he vanished in a cloud of dust.

"I don't think I can take much more," Hal said wearily.

Several million years later, Birch Lake came in sight. It's difficult to skulk through town with a horse and canoe/buggy, but somehow we managed and reached the dam without being seen by anyone.

"I'm so tired I'm gonna sleep for a week," Hal gasped as we wrestled the heavy canoe down the steep bank to its original mooring.

"That's it," he said, as we slid the canoe into the river and tied it securely.

A perverse stubborn streak, which once had prompted my father to comment, "Bobby, you're so muleheaded you wouldn't eat steak in a famine if someone ordered you to do it!" now manifested itself.

"No it isn't," I said. "We still got to get the mailbox back." Hal looked at me incredulously.

"Dump it! Throw it in the river!"

"No," I said mulishly. I was so tired all I wanted to do was lie down and moan. But I was damned if I'd leave a loose end. Not after all that trouble. "I'm going back."

"You're nuts! You're really screwy!" Hal shouted. "Well, scram, nuthead! I'm gonna go home!" He jutted his jaw at me, daring me to say something. I shrugged. Hal stumbled up the hill and vanished. I went back to the buggy. Blackie was showing some weariness himself. He stood, head down, and appeared to be shaking his head and talking to himself.

"Come on, Blackie," I said. "We got to make one more trip." Blackie's lips fluttered despondently.

It was an hour and a half trip to the little house. I wrestled the mailbox back into place, feeling the drained tiredness in my arms when at last it was upright again. They'd wonder where all that grease came from, but then you can't win them all.

Then I got back on the buggy and turned Blackie toward home. He plodded wearily, hoping this was the last trip. His ears drooped and his flanks were white with sweat salt. I got him back in his pasture, put up the buggy, put away the harness, and found a rag and brush and wiped Blackie down.

I leaned my head against his damp neck as I brushed lethargically. "Geez, I'm pooped," I told him. He nickered understandingly. It was twilight.

Very slowly I tottered home where my mother was just beginning to worry about me.

"Oh," she exclaimed, visibly relieved to see me. "I was wondering where you were. Look at your clothes! What a mess! Well, what were you up to today?

"Nothing," I said. "We didn't do nothing, Mom."

THE DAY WE STUNK UP
THE GOVERNOR

I'd have to blame it all on Essie Finley's old single-barrel shotgun with the cracked stock and the pitted bore. The fact that we stunk up the Governor of Wisconsin, I mean.

We wanted the shotgun so badly we hurt and we were abysmally broke. If we had not been too broke to buy Essie's shotgun, we would not have been driven to desperate lengths, lengths which resulted in the stinking up of the Governor.

Stinking up Governors is not bright, whether you agree with them politically or not.

Essie Finley was the Birch Lake town drunk, or one of them. For a small town, Birch Lake had a very liberal stock of town drunks. Essie didn't own much, but he did own the battered shotgun which he was willing to sell for $10.00 (or more than three bottles of the low-cost, high-kick lightning he drank).

There was no limit to the adventures my cousins, Hal and

Frank, and I could enjoy with our own shotgun. "We could shoot squirrels," Frank said.

"We could shoot ducks," Hal said.

"We could shoot grouse," I said.

"Not without no ten dollars," Essie said.

How could we have known that the Governor of Wisconsin would choose that particular hot July day to dedicate the new Birch Lake Courthouse, the architectural pride of northern Wisconsin? To us it was just another day we didn't have enough money to buy that shotgun. The morning was hot enough to turn fat men skinny. We headed disconsolately for the upper end of Birch Lake where a big, flat granite rock jutted into the lake, making a perfect diving platform.

Once more, Essie had refused to extend credit, a position he shared with our parents. "Doggone Essie anyway!" I exclaimed. Every year ducks came into Birch Lake and every year we watched everyone else hunt them. The only hunting we'd been able to do was chunking rocks at chipmunks, and the chipmunks so far had us shut out.

"My dad told me my credit rating would scare a loan shark," I said. "He said I was already into next year's allowance and that if I follow the same fiscal policies when I grow up, I'll probably be President. I don't know what he's talking about except it means we ain't gonna get the ten bucks from him."

Essie had indicated he had a monied sucker on the string and we'd better come up with the scratch quick or the gun would be gone. I daydreamed, almost feeling the hard kick of the gun as a partridge feathered down through the crisp golden chill of autumn. The summer sun dimmed and grew gray as I thought of losing that magic gun.

Then Frank saw the object lying on the heat-shimmered road ahead. "Hey! Somebody ran over something." When we reached the object, we discovered it was a defunct coyote, road-killed long enough before that it had bloated enormously and had reached a state of putrefaction which staggered everything downwind——mostly us.

"Jeez!" Frank cried. "I smelled better stuff at the city dump!"

We suffered until it occurred to us we'd feel better if we moved upwind. Green flies, in a state of bliss, hummed sluggishly around the corpse. Hal studied the dead coyote. "They pay bounties on these things," he mused. "Fifteen dollars bounty."

My eyes widened and my mouth slowly came open. Fifteen dollars meant Essie Finley's shotgun, with money left over for John Wayne movies. We held a reverent wake over our suddenly valuable chunk of carrion.

No one could decide whether we were supposed to cut off ears or scalp (and no one wanted to do it anyway), so we decided to take the whole animal to the courthouse for bounty. I ran back to town for a gunny sack, and when I returned we prodded the animal into it, holding our breaths and trying not to gag. We carried the sack toward town, holding it as far away from us as we could.

We met Essie Finley, weaving toward the tiny shack he called home. He stopped and wrinkled his red, porous nose. "What the hell is that *smell!*" he exclaimed, his yellowy eyes widening.

"It don't matter, Essie," Hal said triumphantly. "You just hang on to that old shotgun!"

The town was silent and deserted. Everyone was at the city limits, waiting for the Governor's motorcade. It was the first time in memory a governor had visited Birch Lake, but then it was the first time Birch Lake ever dedicated a courthouse in an election year, too. We clopped into the echoing foyer of the big, new building, the sack dangling between Hal and me.

"Hey, you kids!" We jumped guiltily and whirled. A man in overalls was bearing down on us. "You get out of here!" he shouted. "The Governor's gonna be here in a couple of minutes."

"We came to bounty a coyote," Hal said stubbornly.

"Not in here you ain't," Overalls said. "Beat it!"

"We want our money," Hal persisted.

"I don't know nothin' about no dead wolves," Overalls snarled. "All I know is if you don't haul yer tails outa here, I'm gonna jerk a knot in 'em!"

"Who does that old grouch think he is anyway," Hal grumbled outside.

"He think's he's bigger than us," I said. "And he's right."

"We're gonna go back in there and get our money," insisted Hal, who had inherited an overdose of our family's most notable trait——muleheaded stubborness.

"Geez!" I protested uneasily. "Suppose that mean old guy catches us? He'd use our guts for garters."

"Chicken! Boy, you're a really one-hundred percent Plymouth Rock!"

I preferred being beaten up to being called chicken, so we crept back to the courthouse which gleamed quietly. We slipped through a basement door and crept upstairs to the main corridor. Then we heard the measured clomp of work boots on the balcony above us. We panicked and bolted through the nearest door.

The room which we entered was ablaze with powerful lights and filled with folding chairs. At the far end was a dais and on it a speaker's stand. A banner, in glittery letters, proclaimed, "Welcome to Birch Lake, Governor!"

"We better get out of here!" I whined, terrified. All I could think of was that my sneakers were torn and my jeans had a hole in the fanny and I was carrying a very dead coyote. Things were beginning to hem us in.

Frank, who had been peeping through the door, turned to us in fright. That big mean guy is comin'!" he bleated shakily. Hal and I grabbed the sack and we sprinted into some sort of storeroom. We detoured around a big piece of machinery——a furnace or something——and cowered in the corner. This clearly was the end of the road. The only door out led straight into the bulgy-muscled, hairy arms of Overalls. "It was all *your* idea!" Hall hissed viciously, forgetting that it was all *his* idea. "If you hadn't hollered so much about that damn dumb old shotgun!"

"Hey, Homer!" called a far-off voice. "They're comin'!" Almost instantly the auditorium was filled with many voices as the crowd pushed in and found chairs, with much clatter and banging. It was stifling hot.

A voice said, "Let us rise for the invocation." Frank and Hal and I scrambled to our feet and bowed our heads. After the prayer (I don't know what everyone else prayed for, but I prayed to get out of the mess we were in), the Governor rose to speak. We peeped through the door.

"Mr. Mayor, honored guests, ladies and gentlemen," he began. "It gives me great pleasure to be here on this fine, hot July day" He looked anything but pleased——more like a fat lady with a pinching girdle caught in a traffic jam. His florid face streamed perspiration.

"In fact, Mr. Mayor," the Governor said in a tight aside that was not quite jocular, "where is this fine new air-conditioning system you were bragging about?"

The mayor blushed and made an impatient gesture and, to our horror, we saw Overalls detach himself from the wall and head toward our room. "Geez!" I moaned. "He's gonna come in here!" We ran for the closet, then remembered the sack.

"Stick it somewhere!" Hal hissed. "He'll kill us if he finds us in here!" Frank jerked open a door on the big piece of machinery and we crammed the sack into the opening. With a tired sigh, the bloated animal deflated, loosing a blast of dead animal aroma which staggered Frank. He slammed the panel and stumbled away, green of gill, swallowing noisily.

We fled into the little closet and barely made it as the outer door opened, letting in a tatter of sound.

"Whew!" exclaimed Overalls to himself. "What the hell is that *smell*! Dead mouse probably. Get it later." He threw a switch on the big machine and it grumbled a couple of times, clicked and belched metallically and began to hum. Overalls left and we crept from the closet, weak with fright.

". . . believe I can safely say that this building will go down in history as . . . " the Governor was saying. He faltered and seemed to test the wind, like a bird dog investigating a vagrant scent. He cleared his throat. "Ah, go down in history as . . ."

Once again he paused and rubbed his hand across his nose. A slight shudder rippled over his round body. A rustle of whispers skittered through the audience. Cool air poured into the room through a dozen vents, along with the most horrible stench imaginable. We had stashed our dead coyote in the blower box of the air-conditioning system.

The Governor coughed and gagged slightly. "Put the town on the map . . ." he faltered bravely on. But his face had a pistachio sheen and beads of sweat dotted his brow. ". . . on the map with any town. . . " he muttered. He stumbled a step from the microphone and spoke to no one in particular: "What the hell is that *smell*!"

Someone leaped up, overturning a chair, and cried, "I'm getting out of here!" That did it. Instantly everyone was up, shouting, milling about, and knocking over chairs.

"It's a commie plot!" a woman screamed hysterically. "It's a union stinkbomb!" shouted a local capitalist. Hal and Frank and I looked at each other with eyes as big as all outdoors. If anyone found out about this, the bounty on the coyote would be nothing compared to the bounty on us.

We slipped through the forest of milling people and, in the general confusion, shot through the door and out into the summer sun. We didn't stop running until we reached the big flat rock at the upper end of the lake. All three of us hit the water simultaneously, fully clothed.

We spent the next hour scrubbing our skin and clothing with sand. We paused every so often to sniff each other, then dived back into the cleansing waters of Birch Lake. At dusk, we crept home, expecting to be met by a company of grim National Guardsmen.

Nothing happened.

Nothing except that, as soon as he returned to the Capitol, the Governor issued a stinging denunciation of the outdated predator bounty system and called for the legislature to outlaw wasteful bounty payments.

I guess Frank and Hal and I were the youngest conservation lobbyists Wisconsin ever had. But we never bragged about it.

THE WORLD'S BIGGEST BLUEGILL

Every kid needs a fishing buddy. Uncle Al was mine. A fishing buddy is someone who teaches you to love fishing. He is someone with whom you can crouch in a rocking boat for hours and not be bored, even if the bluegills aren't biting and the lake is rhythmically choppy and you have a chigger bite on your butt that is driving you wild and sweat keeps burning your eyes.

Uncle Al was an unlikely hero. Everyone else in the family considered him a n'er-do-well. Or a n'er-do-*anything* for that matter.

He was faded and wind-battered and he didn't have any teeth and rarely wore his ill-fitting mail order choppers. He drank beer as if it were going out of style and used words that would have made my mother turn pale and faint.

But he taught me how to catch the big bluegills and how to drift fat worms under the alders on Thirty-Three Creek to catch bigger brook trout than anyone else in town. He knew where woodcock rested when they started moving south and how to hunt grouse (and how to hit them regularly with a tattered old double barrel that was barely out of the black powder era).

Maybe my affection for grizzly old Uncle Al was what kept me running with the bucket banging against my leg and water running into my shoes. Then again, it could have been the family trait of pigheadedness.

It all started at Hogan's Garage where five old cronies gathered every morning to argue. "Sounds like old lady Humphrey has got sick valves there," commented Cricket Crockett, listening to the clatter of a car Hogan was working on.

"Sick valves my flaming fuzz," sneered Tight Line Trotter. "If that ain't a grindy transmission, I'll eat buzzard guts for a week!"

I sat quietly in a corner on an overturned grease bucket, listening to them argue. Mostly they didn't know what they were talking about, but there was one subject on which they all really were expert, and that was bluegill fishing.

Crickett Crockett got his nickname because he used nothing but crickets for bait. He regularly toured every damp basement in Birch Lake, turning over old boards and clammy piles of newspapers to expose the blinking bugs underneath.

Tight Line Trotter scorned the bobber. "I want to *feel* them little boogers bite," he declared. There was Grub Harrison who almost slobbered when he was spearing a bee moth grub on the end of a no. 10 hook.

None of them would ever admit it, but they all knew Uncle Al was the best fisherman in the bunch. There wasn't a one of them who wouldn't have given nearly all he owned (in every case not very much) to humiliate Uncle Al in a fishing showdown. Uncle Al didn't have much in life, but he had a knotty self-respect that didn't need trampling on.

"'Spect I'll go bluegillin' this afternoon," said Bitty Bobber Bates, an advocate of miniscule floats. He squinted skyward as if to confirm the balmy nature of the day, a difficult trick since we were inside a windowless concrete block building. Cricket Crockett spat under old lady Humphrey's Ford, which groaned with the pain of its grindy transmission.

"Might be good. I got to get me some crickets, though."

"Any man that'd use crickets would suck eggs," remarked Tight Line Trotter for the sake of argument.

"Oh yeah!" Crockett responded hotly. "You'd use chicken guts if bluegills'd bite on 'em."

"And I'd catch bigger fish than you eight days out of the week, you scrawny little bug chaser!" They glared at each other, breathing heavily.

"Boys, boys," Uncle Al soothed, with a patronizing smile rendered ineffective because his teeth weren't in. "You can piddle around with them black grasshoppers and little bitty weevils and like that, but I'm willin' to bet this little old peewhacker and me can go out with a bait o' worms and catch a bigger bluegill than anyone here."

I blushed as the men looked at the peewhacker, who was me. "You willin' to put yer mouth behind some money, Al?" challenged Crockett.

Uncle Al hesitated, for he and money were almost total strangers. But he had confidence in his skill and besides he couldn't resist a challenge. So he leaped on his high horse and galloped right out to the end of a long limb.

"Yer dern tootin'!" he exclaimed. "Put ten apiece in the kitty and winner take all. The peewhacker here, he's a sprout, so I'll chip in half a buck for him. Okay?"

They all glowered at Uncle Al, pretty sure he was going to take their money, but there was always the chance that he'd have a bad day or they'd have an exceptionally good one. My chance of winning was about in the same proportion as my contribution to the pot.

The five fishermen decided to fish intensively the next day, then report in the morning after at Hogan's with their biggest fish, winner take all. What's more, the losers had to cook the losing fish filets and buy the beer. The winner could sit back on a grease bucket, watch the losers cook, drink their beer, and chortle. Uncle Al could chortle better than anyone I ever knew. He was a bad winner.

Uncle Al chortled as we headed toward my grandmother's barn where he dug all his worms. "That fifty bucks will buy me a case of beer and you a case of sody and we'll have cash left over fer sinkers and shotgun shells and wild, wild woomen!" he cackled. Uncle Al was confident. When it came to bluegill fishing, Uncle Al could have showed Harry Truman a thing or two about cocksureness.

We reached the spot behind the barn where several generations of milk cows had stood placidly mulling their cuds and creating a fantastically rich soil which teemed with fat, muscular earthworms. This heap of humus lay in a maple grove and the compost of leaves and cow outfall had created the richest worm home in Wisconsin. There were some worms in it that could whip a barn black snake two falls out of three.

"When I pitch one o' these here wigglin' porkchops in Birch Lake," Uncle Al said, with a cavernous grin, "them bluegills'll beat each other bloody to get at it."

And, indeed, so it seemed. Within seconds after he'd anchored off his favorite weed bed the next morning, he had a chunky bluegill vibrating on the end of his whippy cane pole. It weighed half a pound and a filet from it, fried in deep fat after having been rolled in beer batter, would make me salivate like a junkyard dog in a butcher shop. "Piddly little thing wouldn't do for pike bait," Uncle Al sneered, for he was after heft in the singular, not the cumulative. He wanted the bull stud bluegill, not his sons and daughters.

Then it happened. His cork plopped under, sending water shooting six inches in the air. The end of the pole dipped sharply and the boat rocked as Uncle Al hauled back, setting the hook in something a solid as my Aunt Alice's pancakes.

The line hissed through the water in big circles, cutting a tiny wake like the fin of a shark. Once Uncle Al thought he'd lose his fish when it swam under the boat. "Come back outa there, you big bastard!" he roared, holding the pole half under the water, hanging out of the boat like the Durango Kid hanging under his saddle to avoid Indian arrows.

The fish began to give ground and finally Uncle Al had his prize laid in the bottom of the boat. It was the biggest bluegill I'd ever seen. It had to weigh at least two pounds.

"Let's go home, old fishin' buddy!" Uncle Al cackled. "If I live to be two hundred, I ain't never gonna catch a bigger one! Can't you see ol' Crockett when I spring this on 'im? He'll be mad enough to chew washers off a rainspout."

We put the fish in a live box at our dock and Uncle Al went up town to quaff a cool one. He intended to be mysterious and to gloat if any of his cronies showed up. I had an afternoon to fill. Well, I still had most of a can of good worms and a half-dollar stake in the pot. Even if I couldn't win, I had the right to try.

There was a twisty half-mile narrows between Birch Lake and Balsam Lake. No one ever fished there because there was a constant daytime stream of boat traffic between the two lakes. Stopping a boat to fish was like changing a tire in the middle of the highway.

But there was a sweet, quiet time of late evening when all the boats were home. It was a magic few minutes when the sun rested on the horizon and the lake waters quit their restless tossing and became content. Cabin doors slammed audibly a mile away. Bee martins and swallows flickered through the deepening shadows after insects. The slosh of a feeding bass carried clearly to me down the darkening narrows as I slithered down a steep, tree-covered hill to a little rock outcrop over the narrow waterway. I wiped a faint film of sweat from my forehead. The narrows was almost entirely shadowed, but the golden rim of the ebbing sun retained a fingerhold on the horizon and lined the bottoms of black-topped clouds with coppery beauty.

I tapped the bait can sideways on the rock to loosen the dirt. One of the powerful worms rolled to the surface. I grabbed him and wrestled him onto my hook. Then I set the bobber about three feet up the line and carefully lobbed it and the baited hook over the bank-hubbing lilypads. Ripples tiptoed away from the bobber.

We sat there, the evening and I, in companionable silence for about 10 minutes. Then there was a cautious tug on my bait and the bobber nodded a warning. Whatever was there wasted no time. The cork shot out of sight and my old casting reel screamed with the discomfort of its years. I thumbed it and hauled hard on the 20-pound test line. It was impossible to stop the initial rush of the fish. My short steel rod wasn't much more flexible than a fireplace poker, but it bent severely and my thumb scorched painfully as the fish yanked out line.

I stopped the first rush, then reeled frantically as the fish bore back toward me. Damn! I'd lost him! No! He was still there. I talked to that fish "Don't get off, fish!" I pleaded, for I knew he was a whopper. "Let me see you anyway."

Gradually I gained a little ground, finally hauled the fish to the surface where it lay on its side and looked at me with what appeared to be a disgruntled expression. It had to be a bluegill, but I looked at it for a long time before my mind would accept what I was seeing.

This was the biggest bluegill on earth. It was a third again as big as the one Uncle Al had caught and, as I stared at the glossy, blue-black back, the brilliant orange chin, the more excited I became. Great day! What had I done! I'd caught the biggest bluegill in all the world! I began to walk home, carrying the mighty fish on a stringer at my side, then I trotted and finally I was running and whooping like a berserker.

But when I reached the house, I slowed down, breathing hard. I wanted, in the worst way, to dash inside and flop the monster fish down in the middle of the supper table, but it occurred to me that the triumph would be all the sweeter if I could spring it on Uncle Al in front of his Hogan's Garage cronies the next morning. It would take all my self-control not to blurt out something, but I decided to cache the fish and keep quiet. I put it in a bucket of water. It was dark now and cicadas filled the soft summer night air with gentle rasp.

It was a family dinner. "Can't hardly wait to see them fellers when I haul in that fish," Uncle Al was crowing to the rest of the family. "They're gonna squirm like frog legs in hot grease!"

Yeah, I thought, and you'll squirm, too, when I cover your fish with mine. Fifty dollars! I couldn't believe it. There was a bicycle down at the hardware store and the fishing rod that I'd been leaving nose prints on the window looking at, and dime Baby Ruths, and Durango Kid movies. There was no end to the luxuries fifty dollars (and fifty cents) could bring me.

"Ain't no way I could get beat," Uncle Al declared, shoveling a heaping forkful of sauerkraut into his mouth. It looked like someone pitching hay into a cave. "No way."

It took me a long time to go to sleep that night. I kept remembering the sharp "plop!" of the bobber as it went under, the bruising pull of the big fish as it bucked in circles, trying to escape the nagging tug at his gristly lip.

The morning was glittery. I raced out behind the shed to check on my fish. He peered up at me companionably. I changed the water because a fish that big sucks a lot of oxygen and I didn't want to risk him dying.

The big bucket was heavy, but my bluegill wouldn't fit in anything smaller. I headed for Hogan's Garage with water slopping over the edge of the bucket and soaking my leg. I stopped halfway at the Town Hall pump for a refill. My bluegill was swimming in very tight circles. He was as big as the bottom of the bucket and couldn't do anything else. I grinned joyfully at him, all fifty pretty dollars of him. "Hang on, old fish," I whispered. "You pretty old fish!"

Shyness stopped me at the garage door. I set the bucket in a shady place beside the building and wiped my damp hands. My shoulders ached from carrying the big fish.

The five contestants were sitting in a circle, arguing hotly when I slipped through the door. The smell of ripening fish was winning over the usual garage smell of oil and grease.

"Git the scale, then, Crockett, you scratchy old fleabag! If mine ain't bigger than that little old minner you got there, I'll chew up yer mungery overalls and swaller them buttons and all!"

"It don't really matter, "Uncle Al said smugly. He produced his slab-sided bluegill from a folded newspaper. "This here one eats yer kind fer breakfast."

There was a low whistle in the chagrined silence that followed. Uncle Al positively glowed with delight.

Now, of course, was the dramatic moment for me to leap up like Perry Mason and cry, "Just a moment, your honor, I believe we have a surprise witness." Then I would produce my fish and we all could enjoy Uncle Al's humiliation while I stuffed the $50.50 in my pocket. I started to say something then shut up as I thought how I wouldn't have known enough to catch my bluegill if it hadn't been for Uncle Al taking me with him, patiently overlooking my iron-thumbed approach to hook baiting, who told me bawdy jokes, who asked my opinion on things——not to be condescending, but because he really wanted to know.

I looked at the seamed back of his neck and what I could see of his stubbly jaw where his salt-and-pepper hair fuzzed over the back of a none-too-clean collar, and I thought, I'll be go-to-hell if I'm gonna do that to my old fishing buddy.

So I slipped back outside and picked up the bucket and started carrying it toward the lake, two blocks away. My already sore muscles groaned, but I ignored them. The bucket banged against my leg and water seeped coolly into my sneakers.

Then I heard Uncle Al yell behind me. "Hey, Bobby! Hey sprout! Looka here what we won!" I walked faster, trying to pretend I hadn't heard him. I glanced back. He was coming after me, holding a sheaf of bills in his gnarled hand. I began to jog. The heavy bucket jounced and my fingers hurt horribly from the strain. "Bobby, hey Bobby! What the hell are you——look what we done!"

Now I was near the lake. If only I could trot down the path to the boat dock and dump the fish before he caught up with me. He was closing in, for he was longer of leg even if one of them was bowed like a wicket from where a spruce log fell on it, and he wasn't carrying the world's biggest bluegill in a bucket.

"Bobby! Yo! Bobby!" We must have looked a sight, me stumbling along with that damn bucket, like someone in a weird handicap race, and Uncle Al gimping along behind me, shouting and waving fifty dollars as if he were trying to buy the bucket. People stopped to look curiously at us. My ears turned red and I breathed hoarsely from the strain. But the most notable trait of our family kept me going——bullnecked stubborness. It also kept Uncle Al chasing me.

"You deef! Damn kid!" he whuffed like a fading engine, but now was so close I could hear him muttering to himself. In another moment his horny hand would close on my shoulder and I would hear him say,"What you got in that bucket?" and then I wouldn't be his kid fishing buddy anymore. I'd just be another competitor.

I grabbed the bottom of the bucket and flung the fish into the lake. The water hung in the air for a long moment, outlining the massive fish. There was a splash and the biggest bluegill in the world disappeared.

"What the hell!" Uncle Al growled.

"It wasn't anything, Uncle Al," I babbled desperately, turning toward him. I was shaking all over. "It was just a little old rock bass that died."

Uncle Al looked at me and his faded yellowy eyes narrowed and he clamped his toothless jaws together so tightly his nose almost hooked under his chin. I tried to put all the love I felt for him into the look I gave him. He squinted at me forever.

Someone started a motorboat across the lake. A car horn blatted. A martin chittered overhead. Life went on.

"You little snake-sided runt!" Uncle Al rasped. He scratched his stubbly jaw with the sheaf of $10 bills. I hung my head, for I was sure my fishing buddy was no more.

"I been trying to catch you so's we can go back up to the hardware store and get you that rod and reel outfit you been moonin' for," he rumbled. "That mangy old outfit you been fishin' with wouldn't catch flies if you coated it with cowflop."

His face was crinkled like it always was when he was telling me one of his outrageous whoppers. I never did know for sure if he knew what I'd done, but that's the nice thing about having a fishing buddy. It doesn't matter.

DOWNHILL ALL THE WAY

The Birch Lake Rialto movie thater had drafts gusting through it like a wind tunnel. In July, it was as stuffy as a high school locker room, but in December——when winds swept across Canada directly off the polar ice cap, funneled down the chain of lakes north of town, howled along Main Street and through the tin sides of the Rialto——it took a strong person with a good set of ear muffs to last through a John Wayne plains epic.

Only my lifetime hero, John Wayne, could have enticed me to the Rialto that fateful late December afternoon with the polar winds whistling and my cheeks chapping.

But it was some obscure Olympic trials finalist named Dieter Something-or-Other who sent me home, eyes shining with more than the effects of a --37° wind chill index, determined to become the world's greatest downhill skier and win the hand of beautiful Janie Prescott, in that order.

Dieter the Bold was featured in a Movietone News Report

which started just as I returned to my seat from the popcorn stand. The popcorn was like eating fried creek gravel. I loved it.

Flashing the famed Austrian smile that had turned several continents full of lovely girls to mush, Dieter jump-turned and sped past the camera in a swirl of snow. "Gee!" hissed my cousin Hal. "Ain't it amazin' what they do with a bent bed slat!"

I scarcely heard him. I was electrified as Dieter the Bold slalomed by at 65 mph. Skiing was a whole new world to me. Even though Birch Lake got six feet of snow every winter, I didn't know a ski from a musk ox. I'd never even been to the Hardpan ski area 15 miles away. My folks were hard-pressed enough to provide me with John Wayne movie admission, much less to shell out money for lift tickets.

I'd just gotten contorted into my favorite viewing position, knees on the back of the seat in front, when someone wanted past. Grunting like an old man, I struggled upright and looked to see who it was. Oh, my! It was Janie Prescott, the girl of my dreams, the girl whose very proximity turned me to Jell-o casserole. Janie had looked expectantly at me a time or two in school, as if she were waiting for a converstional gambit that would make her think she'd found the Birch Lake Charles Boyer. But so dumbfounded was I by her awesome charm that I stammered and finally blurted that our pigs had scours. Another time I dropped all my books and when I finished picking them up and looked around, she was gone.

Janie sat four rows over and three seats up. She had the most beautiful back of the head I've ever seen. I lurched to my feet, showering Hal with my pebbly popcorn. "Hi, Bobby," trilled my vision, squeezing past me so near that I smelled the cold, clean scent of her honey hair. "Can we sit here?"

Janie was with Pamela Potter whose most notable achievement to date had been that she'd gotten acne before anyone else in her peer group. "Yeah!" I exclaimed. "I mean, gosh, yeah!" The old silver tongue continued to be mostly dross. Janie moved two seats over (curses!) and drifted delicately to rest. Pamela fell into the seat next to me like a pole-axed sow and gave me the toothy smile of a horse with an itchy lip.

I shuddered.

Dieter the Bold shattered another pristine slope, the rush of the skis testing the Rialto's antique war-surplus sound system.

Hal leaned over. "Don't get carried away, Love," he whispered.

"All that beauty next to you." I elbowed him in the ribs and he went, "Uhhhhh! uhhhhhhhhh!" for quite a while. Dieter the Bold shot off the lip of an overhang, arcing through space like some graceful bird of prey. He vanished in a cloud of powder, then exploded out of it, his skis singing a paean to the glory of winter sports.

"Isn't he marvelous!" Janie whispered to Pamela as my ears flapped with the effort of eavesdropping. I glanced across Pamela's muzzle and saw the shining eyes of my Beloved. Her rosebud mouth was delicately agape as she marveled at Dieter the Bold. A pink tongue played gracefully across bee-stung lips. I ached with unrequited love. If Janie wanted skiers, then my new hero was Dieter the Bold. Sorry, John Wayne, but that's the way the heroism crumbles.

Pamela, her attention caught by my gawping gaze across her bow, gave me another equine grin and I tumbled to earth like a shot sparrow. Oh, if only I could ski! I'd slalom down the slopes right into Janie Prescott's tender heart! If only I could ski, I'd sweep her off her elfin feet and we'd traverse into the golden sunset.

If only pigs had wings, they could fly.

As we left the theater, I was plunged in despair. How could I learn to ski and win the fair Janie? Ahead of me, Janie paused, her lovely honey hair receiving the gentle comfort of a red-knot stocking cap to keep it from becoming chilled by Birch Lake's bitter cold. "She sure does like those skiers, doesn't she," I muttered moodily, voicing my half-formed fantasy.

"She likes Ricky Turner," sniffed Pamela Potter beside me. I jumped. She sneered at me. "He plays bebop on the trumpet." She looked at me as if I were a sow bug. "What can you do?"

Pondering on it, the only positive talent I could think of was my ability to swallow air and belch on request.

I trudged through a snowstorm toward home. Powder, they called it. New snow. I slid my feet experimentally, slipped, and fell heavily. I tried it again, could almost feel the skis on my feet, a part of me as I negotiated sheer pitches, slalomed winding woodland trails, rode mogulled slopes with piston-kneed skill.

But fate was in my corner. Or, come to think of it, fate was in the other corner. But fate did enter. It was a want ad in the Birch Lake *Chronicle*.

"Wanted: Boy to work during Christmas holidays at Hardpan ski area." I leaped from the chair with a wild cry and raced to the phone, while my mother picked up the pieces of the dish she had dropped when I yelled, and my father muttered and mopped hot coffee out of his lap.

Mr. Davidson, the manager of the ski area, said he'd give me a try and would pick me up the next morning. "Watch out, Dieter Phoney-Baloney!" I exulted. "Here I come!"

Mr. Davidson was a harassed-looking man who gnawed a cold cigar voraciously like a dog chewing a knuckle bone. "Okay, kid," he said, his eyes roving harriedly over the packed ski lodge as if he were afraid the milling skiers might suddenly riot and wreck the place. "You shuffle hot dogs and soda pop until about three. After that, things kind-of thin out and it's okay with me if you check out an old pair of boots and skis and play around 'til time to go home. You do ski, don'tcha?"

"Er, oh yeah!" I lied. My dreams coming true! I ticked off the timetable. A couple of days to get my sea, er, ski legs, then on Saturday I could invite the luscious Janie to visit Hardpan and I'd come blasting down the hill and spray to a graceful stop in front of her. I could see her love-flushed face and hear her exclaim, "Bobby! You're marvelous!" Let Ricky Turner top that with his crummy trumpet. I'd jerk a knot in his stiff upper lip!

Mr. Davidson's operation wasn't exactly top drawer. His only lift was a rope tow, operated by a Model A truck perched atop the hill, jacked up so the rear wheels were off the ground. He started the engine each morning with a fearful assortment of groans, pops, minor explosion, and shrieks, some of which emanated from the truck and some from Mr. Davidson. A thick rope ran around the rear wheel rim and snaked down the slope through the bushes and timber. At the bottom of the slope, you grabbed the rapidly moving rope and hoped it didn't jerk your arms out of their sockets. At the top, the rope soared 15 feet in the air, around a large wheel, thence back to the Model A drive unit.

There were skilled platoons of skiers flitting down the slope when I diffidently carried my battered old skis out of the lodge. Mr. Davidson didn't furnish the help with Olympic-caliber equipment. I think my stuff had last been used by a Finnish soldier protecting Helsinki from the Nazis.

All around me people were skiing effortlessly. I felt intimidated and afraid to put the skis on the clumsy, stiff boots.

There was a small crowd around the bottom of the rope tow and I clumped off to one side to don my skis. I stepped into the right ski which immediately drifted out from under me. I sat down in the snow, with my foot trapped in the binding, bent painfully forward.

"Hey, kid, you okay?" A Greek god in tasteful ski garb towered above me. He was all muscles and white teeth.

"Yeah," I babbled. "I'm just——er——stretching my ligaments." What a stupid thing to say! Muscles gave me a peculiar look through his ski goggles and shook his head. He grabbed the slithering rope and shot up the slope out of sight. Somehow I struggled to my feet, like someone trying to escape from quicksand, and there I tottered. It was like trying to walk a tightrope wearing snowshoes.

After a few minutes, the crowd began to evaporate, driven home by fatigue, incipient darkness, and the biting cold that fell in as soon as the sun showed signs of quitting for the day. It was time for me to strut my stuff, such as it was. No one to watch critically, no one to laugh at my errors. The sun now was but a frosty ghost over the horizon, a chilly illusion, like a mother-in-law's smile.

The lift was clear and I poled over to it as awkwardly as a mallard walking on ice and lined up with the flying rope. I took a deep breath, grabbed the rope and popped right out of the bindings. But for some idiotic reason, I didn't let go of the rope. So there I was, being dragged up the hill like someone tethered to a stampeding elephant through two feet of snow, while my skis remained exactly where they had been.

I finally came to my senses enough to let go of the rope. I plowed to a halt. After I brushed packed snow from my stinging face, I saw Muscles standing over me again. "Look, kid," he said. "You don't know any more about skiing than the Pope knows about playing second base. Let me show you a couple of things." I nodded miserably. My dreams of impressing Janie Prescott with my skiing so far were shaping up about as realistically as my idea of impressing Margie by driving a road grader.

Muscles showed me how to lean backward into the rope tow and away we went, me in front, wobbling like a bottle rocket, Muscles behind, ready to field me if the tow fungoed me.

We came to the top where I was to release the rope, coast to a halt and wait for further instruction. "Let go!" Muscles called from somewhere behind me. Only somehow I had become entangled with the rope and couldn't let go. As the brow of the hill fell away, the rope soared to its pulley wheel. And so did I. I felt myself become airborne. "Let go!" Muscles screamed.

Up, up, up, I went. Then I hit a safety bar and it threw the mechanism out of gear and everything stopped. There I dangled, 10 feet above the ground.

The lift operator came out of his little heated shack, grumbling about "green kids oughta stay offa the slope if they don't know what they're doin'," and other endearments calculated to make me feel as dumb as a backward chicken. Muscles slapped me on the back. "Hang in there," he said. But I don't think he meant literally. There were very few people on the slope now.

The lodge and the emptying parking lot were far below us, miniaturized by distance. The slope was a white blanket spread in front of me. I gulped. It sure was high. The vastness and sharp pitch of the hill frightened me and I sufered sudden vertigo, a total disorientation. I fell over on my side. My face was spending more time in the snow than a snowflake. Muscles hauled me to my feet. "Geez, kid," he said. "What do you want to learn to ski for anyway?"

"There's this girl, " I admitted haltingly.

"Ah!" he exclaimed knowingly, "might have known. Look, if you want to impress some chick, why don't you learn to play the trumpet?"

I snarled and jerked away from him. Surprised, he lost his balance and fell. Before he could right himself and stop me, gravity seized my skis and they began to move downhill.

I discovered a basic law of ski physics immediately——you can go faster than you want to go within the blink of an eye. The hill began to blur as I picked up speed and I was buffeted by air resistance. I hurtled down, faster and faster, with no idea how to stop. Panic numbed my brain. It didn't occur to me at first to fall down, and when it did I was going so fast I was afraid to do it. Once I crossed a small hummock and sailed through space for a heart-stopping instant, then slammed to earth. I didn't know what to do. I didn't know how to turn or how to stop.

Ahead of me was the ski lodge, its warm lights yellow and inviting in the near darkness. Mr. Davidson was inside the building toward which I plunged, gnawing his cigar apprehensively and expecting catastrophe. With good reason.

"Snowplow! Snowplow!" shouted Muscles somewhere in the dimness behind me. I thought it was some kind of cute nickname he had picked for me and I keened in terror, teetering on the brink of lost balance. The cold air stung my eyes and made them tear. My skis chattered and spat on the hard-packed snow. I must have been going close to fifty miles an hour.

Racks of skis and poles fronted the lodge. There was a set of huge swinging doors leading into the lodge and I headed for them as surely as an arrow from the bow of a champion. All I could do was to hang on to my fragile thread of balance and pray for a miracle. Why would anyone want to build a lodge at the base of a hill where dumbheaded skiers could run into it?

The sounds of group singing wafted into the frosty air as I rocketed closer to the lodge. "Oh, there's blood on the saddle, and blood on the ground. . . ." It lent a very ominous note to the situation.

I squirted between the ski racks and my ski poles snagged on either side. Luckily the retaining straps were old and weak or I would have broken both wrists.

But the straps broke instead and the jolt straightened me up just as the ski tips hit the doors, flinging them explosively inward. The skis stopped instantly, but I didn't.

I catapulted forward as the bindings released with the sound of a gunshot.

My racing brain registered a montage——a long table of apres-ski revellers directly in front of me, a guitar player in a bulky sweater facing me at the foot of the table, the warming fire crackling cheerfully, Mr. Davidson behind the cash register, his frayed cigar dropping from his lip in superslow motion.

Then I spread-eagled on the table, like a crippled fighter plane pancaking onto the deck of an aircraft carrier. I surfed the length of the table, scattering hot dog, drinks, and skiers like startled quail. The man with the guitar dodged to one side, but for some inexplicable reason handed me the guitar as I sailed past. I shot off the far end of the table like a stone skipped off a lake surface and went into a reflexive tuck over the guitar.

I hit a big easy chair at about twenty miles an hour, bowling it over. I somersaulted off it into a sitting position on an oval braided throw rug and, like the hero of an Arabian Nights story, coasted across the smooth floor to a gentle stop at Mr. Davidson's feet. The strings of the guitar vibrated in gentle discord.

"Mr. Davidson," I said, my voice quavery in the thick silence, "can I get a ride home with you?"

It was dark in Birch Lake when Mr. Davidson made the turn onto Main Street. I huddled on the passenger side, every muscle in my body hurting. Mr. Davidson silently chewed his cigar. My pay for the holidays would just about cover the skis which had separated into 20 laminations when they hit the door.

There was a stop sign in front of Bamburger's Grocery and there, coming out the door, was Janie Prescott, hand-in-hand with Ricky Turner. Janie was laughing. Ricky was laughing. Ricky was carrying a trumpet case.

Mr. Davidson let me out in front of our house. I climbed painfully from the car. "See you tomorrow, kid," he said, and drove up the snow-covered street. Big flakes of new snow sailed peacefully through the street lights like white moths.

My mother, worrid because of my lateness, met me at the door. "Mom," I said, trying to grin, "I gotta take trumpet lessons. I just gotta"

THE BEST DARN DUCK DOG IN THE WORLD

Before he limped into Uncle Al's life, Sam's idea of high living was finding a ripe garbage can. He'd been kicked and rocked and hollered at. He was underfed and overabused. He had fleas, ticks, worms, a touch of moist eczema, and a deep-rooted suspicion of all things man touched.

Uncle Al and I were gathering greens when Sam limped down the dusty road. Neither of us liked greens ("goddam weeds," as Uncle Al described them), but my grandmother, the supreme court of Birch Lake, had ordered up a mess in her voice of thunder and since we both were convinced she could topple buildings with a concentrated glare, we grabbed rusty butcher knives and a tow sack and took off. "Eating this damn shrubbery gives me the mulligrubs," Uncle Al grumbled. He considered beer the only viable health food.

It was then that we saw Sam hobbling down the road, his tail between his legs, his head low. He saw us and stopped, waiting for someone to chunk a rock at him.

"Hey, old dog," I said. "It's all right. We won't hurt you."

Uncle Al straightened up with a vast popping of bones like cooking popcorn. He was all whisker stubble and sweat. The family considered Uncle Al a n'er-do-well. That wasn't accurate. He fished and hunted and drank beer better than anyone in Birch Lake. It was just work that he didn't do very well. I worshipped him.

"Ain't that the worst lookin' dog you ever seen," Uncle Al rumbled. I looked at the two of them and had the strange feeling that I was looking at twins, discarding the obvious species differences. Uncle Al inhabited holey, faded overalls. His toothless mouth, rimmed by Day's Work residue, lay in a bristly face seamed by sun and wind. He was no beauty.

Sam was a Labrador, though he was so gaunt and dust-whitened he looked more like the ghost of a Lab. Sam sat down to study us. The very tip of his crooked tail swirled tentatively in the hot dust. Perhaps he recognized a couple of kindred souls, a pair of fellow stumblers in the eternal race of life. Maybe he was just tired of dodging rocks.

Uncle Al shambled over to the dog and extended a grimy hand to be sniffed. Sam dutifully smelled it, but mostly he looked up at Uncle Al, trying to read what was written in the faded blue eyes. What he saw there reassured him because the black muzzle popped open and a tongue of astonishing pink leaped free and flopped as he panted.

From that moment the two of them were inseparable, except at night when my grandmother relegated "that worthless dog" to the great out-of-doors. Uncle Al instantly planned to make Sam into the greatest duck dog in the world, but Sam would have none of it. He had found the life for which he had searched so long and so painfully and he intended to make the most of it.

With Uncle Al shooting him a steady diet of pork chop rinds, leftover potatoes and gravy, and other high-quality table scraps, Sam grew fat and sleek and drowsed in the shade, raising a droopy eyelid at Uncle Al's hoarse efforts to arouse him from his Labradorian lethargy.

Lord knows, Uncle Al tried to make Sam a duck retriever. "Come on, Sam, boy! Go get it!" he'd shout at the dog, throwing an old sand-filled sock to which he had pinned the stale wings of a mallard he'd dropped out in his duck marsh the year before.

Sam regarded this silly activity with an expression of dedicated indolence. He sighed heavily and drowsed off. "Dammit, Bobby! I know there's a duck dog hid down there somewheres!" Uncle Al cried in frustration.

"He hides it real good, don't he?" I commented with brutal honesty.

Uncle Al tried everything he could think of. My grandmother had some tame ducks, big, waddly, stupid creatures who spent their days lurching around the back yard, talking to each other in gutteral duckese and preening their yellow, tattered plumage.

"Look here, Sam," Uncle Al instructed the dozing dog. Sam peered with sleepy disinterest. "This here is a duck." He pointed at one of the sloppy, waddling Pekins. "Got to start with basics," he said to me. "Come on, boy! Fetch!"

He scooped up a duck and tossed it halfway across the yard. The duck screamed in outrage and plunged heavily into the dust. Sam yawned. "Albert! What is going on out here!" My grandmother stood cloaked in severe majesty in the back door. "You leave my ducks alone!"

We were pretty sure my grandmother could cap erupting volcanoes and sink large ships of war just by looking at them, so Uncle Al and I decided we'd better lay off the Pekins.

I couldn't understand why Uncle Al was so determined to make Sam a duck dog when Sam so clearly indicated he was nothing more than a sleeping dog the likes of which it was easier to let lie. Then B. O. Bumley stopped by and a lot of things fell into place.

The feud between Uncle Al and Bumley had boiled for more than 30 years. They started hating each other in a logging camp when Uncle Al accidentally dropped a tall spruce on Bumley. Scratched and bleeding, Bumley spoke harshly to Uncle Al, then tried to pry him apart, using a peavey like a giant can opener. Uncle Al was attempting to tag Bumley with the loose end of a length of log chain when the woods boss, an enormous Swede who had no time for young-buck high jinks, beat both of them bloody and made them go back to work.

Over the years if Bumley killed an eight-point buck, Uncle Al didn't rest until he downed a 12 pointer. If Bumley caught a seven-pound walleye, Uncle Al had to come in with two, each of which weighed seven pounds and three ounces. If Bumley shot three wood-cock on a crisp October day, Uncle Al would drop four and bag a ruffled grouse to boot. Uncle Al's brook trout ran two inches longer than Bumley's on the average. Everyone in town knew Uncle Al was a better hunter and fisherman than Bumley, and the knowledge festered in Bumley and made him mean and sour. In addition, he'd beaten Uncle Al for the hand of a buxom Scandahoovian lass many years earlier and what seemed to be a triumph turned bitter when she turned out to have the disposition of a bitch bluegill, all mouth and meanness. Bumley hated Uncle Al.

There was one area where Bumley clearly had the best of Uncle Al. Bumley owned the best Labrador retriever in Birch Lake, perhaps in Wisconsin, a magnificent animal who dominated the annual Birch Lake Fall Retriever Trials the way George Halas dominated the Chicago Bears. Each time Bumley collected the top trophy in the Trials, he singled out rumpled, dogless Uncle Al in the crowd and leered evilly at him. It turned Uncle Al's day to ashes, but he couldn't stay away.

One late summer day we were in the back yard trying to coax Sam into some sort of activity typical for a retriever when, with a rattle and a bang like a barrel of dishes falling down a stairwell, Bumley drove his pickup in the drive and stopped.

"What're you tryin' to do, Al?" Bumley sneered, his raspy voice as charming as a copperhead bite. "Training that flea hotel to find his food dish?"

Uncle Al's seamed neck turned a bright red and he would have ground his false teeth if he'd been wearing them.

"He's a real dandy all right," Bumley scoffed. "How'd you get him——the dog pound reject him?" He whooped and slapped his grease-stained overalls. Uncle Al growled.

"Bumley, if you ain't gone in five seconds, I'm gonna beat the hell out of you." Uncle Al favored the direct approach.

"You and what army?" spat Bumley. His forte was not quick repartee. They stood, Uncle Al's spongey nose to Bumley's collarbone, both with fists clenched. Sam closed his mouth and raised his head, a certain alertness tensing him.

"That mutt couldn't find a duck in a bucket," Bumley snarled. Sam walked lazily over to sniff Bumley's leg and Bumley grouched, "Get away from me, you egg-suckin' mutt!" He booted Sam in the ribs and Sam yelped and shied away.

Uncle Al took a wild swing at Bumley and Bumley blocked it, jerked free, and caught Uncle Al with a looping right high on the head. Uncle Al hit the deck with a thud that brought dust boiling up from under the seat of his britches. His normally watery eyes sprinkled more fiercely than usual.

Sam's eyes got big and his ruff roused spikey and stiff. He snarled fearsomely and came at Bumley, with bared fangs. He leaped for Bumley's throat and Bumley decked him, just as he had decked Uncle Al. He completely cold-cocked poor old Sam. The dog flopped to the dust, twitching.

Bumley glared at all of us, turned on his heel and marched back to his truck. "We'll get even with you somehow!" I piped at his burly back. "You big bum!" Bumley stopped, his eartips going white, and I thought, oh, boy, he's gonna come back and plant me, too! But after a moment, he jerked open the pickup door and backed out in a clatter of metal and a spray of gravel. Uncle Al got up, rubbed the lump on his head, and went to see about Sam, who was just coming to, glassy-eyed and whining.

Uncle Al cradled the mutt's head in his lap and gently stroked the dog's sore jaw. He put his stubbly cheek down to Sam's hairy black one and petted him. I turned away, embarrassed.

After that, Uncle Al said no more about making Sam a duck dog. Summer turned to autumn and the nights carried an overtone of winter on a wind that often came from the north. The birches yellowed and flamed briefly before standing naked and white against the gray of the less ostentatious forest.

The Fall Retriever Trials drew near. Everyone knew Bumley and the majestic Duke would walk off with the top trophy, but there was considerable speculation and betting on the order of finish after that.

Retriever Day dawned warm and sultry. Indian summer. A warm rush of moist air came up from the south, colliding with the impatient winter beast waiting to the north, over the lakes and spruce woods. Dark thunderheads brewed and muttered threateningly to the west. "Hope it rains the whole goddam thing out," Uncle Al grumbled. But he really didn't. Even though he'd shrivel inside during Bumley's annual triumph, he couldn't bring himself to stay away.

There wasn't much equipment involved in the Trials. There were two men in a bobbing rowboat with a cage full of wing-clipped tame mallards. The dog owners stood on the end of the town dock with their animals. At a signal, one of the men in the boat tossed a duck in the air while the other fired a blank-loaded shotgun. As the duck splashed down, the dog was signalled after it and was graded on how well he performed the retrieve. If there were any doubts, there were recalls and work on doubles.

Uncle Al stood disconsolately at the rear of the crowd as the trials got underway. He rinsed his mouth occasionally with beer, trying to erase the bitter taste of Bumley's inevitable triumph. Sam drowsed at his feet, oblivious to the excitement.

The first entrant stood nervously at pier end, his retriever quivering excitedly beside him. The duck went up, the gun boomed, the duck splashed, and the dog sailed into the water. The duck paddled furiously. Just as the dog reached out to grab the duck, it dived. The confused dog continued in a wide arc until he reached shore well down the lake from the dock. While his red-faced owner slunk off the dock and the crowd hooted and whistled, the dog shook himself vigorously and trotted toward home.

"Maybe old Sam ain't the best duck dog in the world," Uncle Al muttered, "but he sure oughta be able to beat that."

Bumley was contestant number five, beefy, cocksure, arrogant. The magnificent Duke stood beside him confidently. Duke was the consummate pro, calm, self-possessed, sure of his considerable talents.

Sam lay at Uncle Al's feet perhaps twenty yards from Bumley. The reedy voice of the mallards awoke no lust for duck-getting in his Labradorian heart. It awoke nothing, including Sam. He dreamed on——probably dreaming of taking naps.

Bumley turned and caught Uncle Al's eye. They looked at each other for a long moment, then Bumley let a superior smirk slither across his face, a maddening smile that made Uncle Al growl deep in his throat. Perhaps it was this sound which roused Sam. The dog opened his eyes and looked questioningly at Uncle Al. Then he laboriously hauled himself to a slumped sitting position and began to scratch half-heartedly at an imagined flea.

In mid-scratch, he froze, his body going taut. He was looking at Bumley. In the brief silence which preceded the release of Bumley's duck, I heard a low rumble which at first I thought was thunder from the rapidly approaching storm. But then I realized it was coming from Sam's throat. Deep down, far back, where the atavistic killer prowled restlessly.

The duck went up, the gun boomed, and Sam broke from his sitting position like an unleashed greyhound. He covered the twenty yards in a couple of seconds. Bumley heard the rapid click of claws and a savage snarl and turned just as Sam leaped. The mighty Duke, unstrung by the uproar, his programming thrown into confusion, turned and bit his master on the leg.

Bumley howled, Sam snarled, and the storm thundered.

Sam hit Bumley amidships and all three of them tumbled into Birch Lake with a tremendous splash. Bumley, weighted by the big dog hanging on his leg, went down like a rock. Sam's momentum carried him far out into the water. All he saw when he looked around him in the choppy water was the duck which loosed a panicky squawk and tried to spring into the air.

Evidently the wing clip had not been thorough enough to make the duck completely flightless, for it got off the deck and labored about thirty yards before splashing to an ungraceful landing.

Sam was electrified. His retrieving instincts boomed with the explosive force of a bomb. He was a bringer-in of downed ducks whom neither rain nor snow nor storm of day could stay from his duties.

Sam turned on a surge of dog power and fairly flew through the water. The duck quacked hysterically and again took off on a short flight. Sam bore on. There was a stunning flash of lightning and a deafening thunderclap. The storm which had threatened all morning marched across the lake, dragging a lead-gray wall of rain with it.

Bumley popped up through the surface chop, sputtering and foundering. Duke, realizing it was release and breathe or bite and drown, let go of Bumley's leg, surfaced, and made for shore, a chastened and humbled champion. The men in the duck boat headed for Bumley.

"Never mind that peckerwood!" Uncle Al roared, hopping up and down. "Go get my dog!"

Far out in the lake, Sam churned after the struggling mallard.

"Sam! Come back here!" Uncle Al cried.

The wall of rain beat across Sam and hid him from us. Then it swept across the crowd just as the men pulled Bumley into the boat. Everyone except Uncle Al and I ran for shelter. The wind keened and blew whitecaps on the lake. It rained torrents and the storm shook the old town dock like a pup with a rag doll.

Uncle Al stood on the end of the dock, clutching a support

beam to keep from being blown into the lake, raindrops like bullets battering his whiskery face, squinting into the fury of the storm. Then the storm swept past and the lake slowly subsided. The waves lost their dirty white tops and quieted to gentle riffles.

The lake was empty. There was no sign of Sam. It was more than a mile to the other shore, a long swim for any dog, much less one as out of shape as Sam.

"Come on, Uncle Al," I said. "Let's go home." He continued to glare at the lake. There was nothing I could say. Sam meant more to Uncle Al than anything. Searching for any word of encouragement, I said, "Maybe he made it to Snake Island," though even that tiny pile of rocks almost to the far shore probably was beyond Sam's range.

Uncle Al looked dimly at me, his face glazed with misery. I could see the tiny spark of hope flare. "Come on, Bobby, we're goin' out to Snake Island." He jerked loose the painter on somebody's rowboat, jammed a couple of splintery oars into the locks, and bent into his rowing, pulling the big wooden boat with the strength both of desperation and of a half-century's experience.

I spotted the still, black form at the water's edge even before we reached the pile of rocks and sickly willows they called Snake Island. "He's there, Uncle Al!" I cried. "He's there!" Uncle Al tossed a quick look over his shoulder, then pulled more fiercely at the oars. The boat grated on the rocks and Uncle Al leaped into the shallows and splashed through the rank pickerel weed.

"Is he dead?" I whispered fearfully as Uncle Al knelt by his prostrate dog.

Uncle Al turned toward me, his seamy face streaked by what looked suspiciously like tears, though they may have been lingering raindrops. He gawped a monumental grin at me. "Hell no, he ain't dead, the ornery old buzzard!"

Sam beat his tail very feebly against the wave-rounded rocks. He had the duck gripped firmly in his mouth and the duck also was alive——beaten to tatters, but alive.

"He'd'a' brung it back, too, if we'd'a' give him enough time to rest up," Uncle Al bragged. "This damned old mutt is a sure-enough duck dog."

The judges held a meeting and decided that, while they couldn't give Sam the top trophy since he wasn't even entered, they could recognize him semiofficially (bragging about him in the tavern) as the best dog at the trials.

Bumley went on a five-day drunk during which he loaned Duke to a man from Indiana who promptly disappeared and never was seen again.

"Don't go tellin' me about duck dogs," Uncle Al said firmly, forgetting that even he had given up on Sam. "I know all about duck dogs and I knew all along old Sam was a duck dog."

He whopped Sam on the side, raising a cloud of dust, and the two of them strolled companionably down the street, looking more than ever like twins.

MY UNCLE AL'S GOOD DEED

My Uncle Al may not have been all black sheep, but there was a very definite tinge of gray to him. He was the acknowledged hunting and fishing champion of Birch Lake and had only a couple of enemies in all the world, one of whom was the game warden, a dour prune named Herbert Crinch.

Crinch disliked Uncle Al because he had not been able to catch him in a game law violation (though he certainly had tried often enough). Crinch was not an enlightened game conservator. He figured the hunting and fishing populace was out to job him and, however accurate that may have been, it was hardly the attitude for a public servant. Crinch equated his game warden badge with a royal scepter and treated those whom he encountered in field, forest, or on lake as not-very-loyal subjects. "I'll get you, Al," was his standard greeting to my uncle. "One of these days I'll nail your rusty hide to the barn door."

Not to say Uncle Al never anticipated the walleye season by a day or two or feathered an occasional grouse out of season. But he limited his trespasses to times when he was irresistibly fish or fowl hungry; he didn't shoot out coverts nor catch out trout holes. He understood fish and game biology by gut instinct and he loved the things he shot and caught——they were his life.

Crinch's only visible qualification for being a game warden was zealousness. He never gave up. He was a hatchet-faced little man, mean of manner and mean of mind, possessed of flinty little eyes set so closely in his bullet-shaped head that he looked like a double-barreled .410 gauge shotgun.

Uncle Al's troubles started one warm June night when he had a couple of cool ones at Uncle Floyd's bar and then promised to feed the annual charity picnic of the Birch Lake United Civic Clubs and Good Works Society, a composite of civic clubs, social clubs, ladies auxiliaries and plain party lovers who merged once a year to sell tickets at a dollar apiece to a huge mid-July picnic. The proceeds went to charity.

Hundreds annually showed up to drink beer, consume mountains of smoking ribs, potato salad, pickles, sliced tomatoes, and side dishes of deep-fried bullheads and bluegill fillets. The belching could be heard for miles.

But the owner of the Birch Lake packing house, who had furnished the ribs for the dinner for many years, had inconsiderately died during the winter and the BLUCCGWS was stuck for an entree.

It was at a moment when the planning committee was at a point of desperation that Uncle Al, feeling confident and effusive, clicked his false teeth decisively, gulped half a glass of beer, and elbowed into the worried planning circle.

"I'll furnish the meat," he boasted, talking down all surprised exclamations, intimating he had untapped sources of cookable flesh, implying that he and Oscar Meyer were as close as brothers, hinting that Swift & Co. wouldn't make a move without consulting him.

It was Uncle Al's chance to do something for humanity and to assert himself as a Birch Lake civic leader (an event that even the most optimistic Birch Laker couldn't have dreamed even at the peak of a Bruenig's Lager euphoria).

The next morning, quivering and wretched, Uncle Al was plagued with the nipping terrors. "Honest to hang, Bobby," he moaned.

"I don't know what gets into me sometimes." I knew what it was. It was beer. But I didn't say anything.

It was ebb tide for Uncle Al who sat with his brow in trembly, calloused hands and wondered where he could come by several hundred pounds of prime meat. Herbert Crinch chose that beautiful moment to stop by and chat in his usual friendly manner.

"I heard about that bigmouthed brag down in the bar," he snarled at Uncle Al. "Where do you think you're gonna get enough meat to feed that whole picnic?" He peered suspiciously at Uncle Al. "If you got any plans for jacklighting a deer out of season, you better think again. I'll be on you like a dog on a hamburger, Al. You roll a deer and I'll have you in jail before he stops kicking."

"Go kiss a mink, possum cop," Uncle Al muttered miserably, for the thought of a salt lick and a clandestine rendezvous with a white-tailed deer had crossed his mind.

By the end of June, Uncle Al had caught and iced down enough bullheads and bluegills for the traditional side dish, but he still was embarrassingly short the main course. He couldn't afford to buy a steer and couldn't find anyone fool enough to give him one. "Come on, Al" my Uncle Floyd said, "let us bail you out."

But stubborn pioneer pride, the one trait Uncle Al shared with everyone in the family, made him unable to admit he couldn't deliver on a promise.

"I ain't gonna do it," he said stubbornly, jutting his toothless jaw resolutely. "I'll find something."

He did think of something. "Bullfrogs!" he exclaimed suddenly one hot mid-morning as we rocked gently in his boat on Birch Lake, trying to catch a few more bluegills. "Bullfrogs!"

Mesmerized by sun and gentle wave, I replied instantly, with quick intelligence, "Huh?"

"Bullfrogs. I know where there's a million of 'em. Ain't many this far north. Froglegs, man. Nobody would ever think of somethin' like that. They'd drool like a dog chewin' a toad." He cackled toothlessly. "You wanta go froggin' with me?"

Did I want to go frogging? Did I want a tutti-frutti tank truck? Did I want Melody Hawkins to smile at me? Did I want the schoolhouse to melt?

"You bet!" I you-betted.

My mother was tepid about abandoning me to the somewhat nonchalant care of Uncle Al in the swamps, but didn't want to make an issue of it. She fussed and fluttered, "Now, Al, you be sure Bobby eats his lunch."

"If he gets hungry, he'll eat," Uncle Al growled, stowing his .22 single shot behind the seat of his pickup.

"Do you have to take that gun along?" my mother fretted.

"Unless you want us to jump out the canoe in ten feet of water and swim them bullfrogs down," Uncle Al grouched.

"Well, you be careful now," she twittered.

The Birch River ran through interminable bogs, trackless wastes which would have made a voyageur tremble, before falling off into a series of horrifying rapids where I once nearly lost my cousin Hal. Little tributary creeks slithered across the marshes. There were hundreds of bog holes and sloughs.

There was a big beaver pond a mile or so up one of these tributaries, a spot known only to Uncle Al. It was the mother lode of northern Wisconsin bullfrogs, a veritable Hoptoad Heaven. I scrambled into Uncle Al's canoe, the Birch River Bitch, a huge old wooden craft as agile as a pregnant elephant but big enough to hold a moose.

"Well, gonna gig a walleye or two?" spoke a voice with the grating charm of a frightened cat sliding ten feet down a piece of slate. It was Agent Crinch, hands on hips, glaring down at Uncle Al. He noticed the gun. "Little target practice on shallow-swimming bass maybe?"

"I never gigged a walleye or shot a bass in my life, Crinch, and you know it!" Uncle Al snarled. "I can outfish you any day in the week and I don't need no gig or gun to do it." He thrust his jaw belligerantly out and, because he didn't have his teeth in, his stubbly chin nearly scraped off the bottom of his nose.

"You're up to something. I'll be watching. One of these days I'll get you. One of these days."

"Go gut a carp," Uncle Al suggested. "Go goose a wildcat."

"One of these days," Crinch repeated. He strode up the hill, turned at the top to beam dank sunshine at us with an evil smile, then disappeared.

"Only man I know can sour honey," Uncle Al grumbled.

We swirled out into the Birch River current with Uncle Al jutting his grizzly jaw into the wind, do or die, like Randolph Scott in a Plains crisis.

Later on, Uncle Al maneuvered the canoe with firm skill, threading it up the narrow tributary on which was the bullfrog-infested beaver pond. We drifted into the pond in acute silence.

Uncle Al's eyes roved the reeds for the sight of the calm frogs semisubmerged among the lily pads. I tried to keep quiet and ignore the fact that I had to go to the bathroom. I crouched in the prow, contemplating my plumbing problems as the canoe brushed through the swamp grass with a slight whispery sound.

Suddenly there was a gigantic thrashing in the grass right beside us, violent and explosive. The reeds thrust turbulently aside and I was face to bulbous, hairy face with 1,600 pounds of disturbed and enraged moose.

The moose, looming over me like Mt. Popocatepetl (and just as explosive) glared downward with mean, beady eyes and roared "merlooooooooaaaah!" in a voice which nearly blew me out of the canoe.

"My God!" Uncle Al cried, his jaw dropping like a separated shoulder. The moose, breathing noisily and angrily, gathered itself to trample us into the marsh mud. Uncle Al flipped the .22 to his shoulder in as fine a bit of instinctive reaction as I've ever seen and shot the moose through the temple.

The enormous beast turned glassy-eyed, sagged, then toppled dead into the water with a gargantuan splash which nearly foundered us.

There was an extended silence while the rippling water slowly subsided. I sat and shook as if ghosts were after me. "Kerlumph," commented a sour-faced bullfrog in front of the canoe.

"Sweet cow sweat!" Uncle Al breathed finally, looking at the dead moose which bulked out of the water like a foundered whale. Confronted with 1,600 pounds of defunct moose, my first reaction was to run like hell. But there was no place to go.

In moments of stress, Uncle Al always turned for advice to his favorite counselor. He talked to himself. "Now, just calm down, Al," he admonished himself, rubbing his bristly whiskers with a worried knuckle. "You've got a problem here. Big damn problem. Big, *big* damn problem. You gotta do something about it. That's right, something. All right, what?"

He gummed his lip. "Well, you could just paddle right out of here. Forget the whole thing. But all that beautiful meat. Steaks, roasts, ribs——enough to feed Birch Lake for a month. Great day in the morning!"

Uncle Al looked at me, his mouth gaping like the mouth of

Mammoth Cave, his yellowy eyes glistening with the fire of inspiration. "The picnic," he said, giving me a toothless smile of pure joy.

"But aren't mooses illegal?" I asked. He frowned.

"I dunno," he said. "I ain't never seen one before. There ain't been a moose around here for fifty, sixty years or more."

"Well, maybe if you told the game warden," I began. Fright leaped into Uncle Al's eyes.

"Crinch! That Nazi wouldn't believe me if I told him the sun come up in the east. He'd bury me so deep they'd have to pipe in daylight."

We sat in silence, holding a somber wake over the moose. Finally Uncle Al said, "We got to dress him out. Then we'll tell," he paused and swallowed noisily, "Mama. Maybe she can figure out something."

Uncle Al could field dress a deer in less time than it takes to tell about it, but, confronted with the moose, he had the demeanor of a man about to dismantle the Empire State Building with a mallet and a cold chisel. He didn't know where to start.

Finally the awesome job was done and the moose meat was distributed around the canoe. The craft rode almost to the gunwales, deep in the water, but it floated. "Sit light," Uncle Al advised grimly.

We floated ponderously down to the Highway E bridge. Uncle Al cached the canoe up a shallow, alder-choked slough so it was hidden and we hitchhiked back to Birch Lake.

We got a ride with an elderly farmer who knew Uncle Al (as did everyone in a forty-mile radius).

"Been fishing, Al?" asked the farmer.

"Ah, no. Just taking the boy here on a little boat ride," Uncle Al evaded.

"Ought to get out," the farmer called above the clatter of the truck. "Talked to a man from down to Haugen who said he landed a big musky out of the river a couple of days ago. Big as a moose."

Uncle Al looked sharply at the farmer and appeared to swallow a golf ball. He was pale under the stubble of whiskers——like a cornfield underlain with a skiff of snow.

When we got back to Birch Lake, Uncle Al retrieved the pickup and we drove back to the moose-laden canoe. We stealthily loaded the truck until the rear wheels splayed like a cow standing on ice, then tried to cover the whole incriminating pile with a tarp. Unfortunately, there was more moose than tarp.

Uncle Al said little, thinking dark thoughts of crime and punishment. He munched his wrinkled lips bleakly. We stashed the meat in my grandmother's shed and carried the ponderous hide and antlers far back in the woods behind the pasture and buried them. Then we crept into the house, both bloody and bowed.

My grandmother filled a room like an eagle perched on the mantle. She regarded us with flinty eyes which seemed, to our guilty consciences, all knowing. We stood awkwardly before her like two small boys, rather than one and a grown man. I tried to pretend I was invisible. It never had worked before and it didn't this time.

Uncle Al told her what he had done.

My grandmother looked at him for about two thousand years. Finally she took a deep breath that nearly emptied Birch Lake of air.

"You did *what!*" she exclaimed with Olympian astonishment.

"Mama, I shot a moose," Uncle Al murmured miserably, cringing.

"A moose," she echoed as if she couldn't believe what her ears were saying to her.

"Yes, ma'am," he confirmed. "I was wondering if, I mean, whether you could think, uh, dammit, Mama, I don't know what to do."

My grandmother stood as if stunned. "Mama?" Uncle Al questioned.

"A moose. . . ." She roused herself like a football player shaking off a crushing block. Then she drew up to her full pioneer height, looking remarkably like John Wayne.

"Albert," she said quietly, "you should be whipped." For a taut moment I thought she was going to take her half-century-old son across her knee and blister him.

"Well, I had to or he'da trompled us," Uncle Al whimpered.

"Where is the moose now?"

"Out in the shed," Uncle Al muttered.

"Out in the . . . !" She cast her eyes to Heaven, perhaps seeking the opinion of her peers, then slowly took off her apron. "I'm going to call the family together," she said. "Go in the parlor and sit down. And don't move."

The family gathered in the parlor, an indication of the seriousness of the situation. The parlor was for Sunday and company and extremely serious situations. My grandmother presided like

Thor over an assemblage of Norse deities. Uncle Floyd and Uncle Frank and Uncle George were there, along with a few insignificant cousins, two aunts, my mother and father. Uncle Al and I sat in a corner, miserable and frightened.

"Albert has shot a moose," my grandmother said into an anxious hush. The words fell like bricks on the old flowered rug.

Uncle Floyd recovered first. "There ain't no mooses in Wisconsin. Al's been drinkin' again."

"Have not!" Uncle Al flared. "There may not be no mooses now, but there sure was one a coupla hours ago!"

"There is a moose," my grandmother interjected. "My shed is full of it. The question is: what do we do with it? I suspect it is illegal meat. Albert made an honest mistake and wants to donate the meat to the Good Works Picnic, but he feels and I suspect he's right that the game warden would take the opportunity to treat him poorly."

"He'd gut me like a carpsucker," Uncle Al muttered miserably.

"Geez, Al," Uncle George said sympathetically. "They'd shut you away until the year two thousand."

Uncle Al gummed a knuckle worriedly.

"What about Bobby?" my mother quavered. "Will they put him in reform school?" I wailed in terror.

At that moment of consummate fright, there was a clattering knock at the front door. We all froze, looking at each other as guilty as hell. Uncle Al tiptoed to the front window and peeked through the curtain.

He turned with the expression of a man who has bet his life on four kings only to be shown four aces by the Devil. "It's the game warden!" he whuffled. "He'll lock me up."

The knock sounded again, as explosive as a howitzer barrage in a tile bathroom. The only person not frozen with fear was my grandmother who wasn't afraid of the Wolf Man. "Open the door," she commanded.

Functioning like a rusty mechanical toy, Uncle Al tottered stiffly to the door and slowly opened it. "Okay, where is it?" growled Crinch, looking like a bowl of clabbered milk. Uncle Al could only swallow, his Adam's apple rippling up and down his wattled neck like a yo-yo.

"I got you this time, you old buzzard," Crinch declared. "Somebody saw a deer leg sticking out of the back end of that rusty junk heap of yours. I figure you went out and plugged yourself a nice big fat buck. But we both know they ain't in season. How's that for figuring, Al?"

Uncle Al swallowed some more. Crinch jabbed him with a triumphant glare. "Let's take a look out back, huh? Maybe in the shed?" Before anyone could react, he turned and vanished around the corner of the house, headed for the repository of one thousand pounds of hot moose meat.

The family thundered for the back door like a cavalry charge, except for me (too slow) and my grandmother, who would not have lost her dignity had she been parachuted into the middle of the charge up San Juan hill. When all had cleared a path, she rose and proceeded to the shed at a measured pace.

There was a scalding argument in full bloom by the time she reached the shed. "Well, what is it then if it ain't venison!" Crinch shouted, waving a slightly bloody chunk of moose meat. "I guess I know venison when I see it!"

"It ain't venison," Uncle Al muttered mulishly.

"You'd lie like ten dogs to save your horny old hide. You know damn well it's deer meat."

"'Tis not!"

"'Tis!"

"Be quiet!" The reverberating voice of my grandmother fell on the scene with the dramatic impact of a mountain collapsing. There was instant silence. Even Crinch, who hadn't spent a lifetime quailing before her majestic wrath, grew still and wary. When she spoke, far-off seismograph needles ran off the paper.

"You act like two little boys. Mr. Crinch, the meat is not deer meat." Her evasion was as neat as one I could have come up with and I silently applauded her.

"Not deer meat, my sweet Aunt Fanny!" Crinch shouted, beginning to lose his temper.

"My son is not lying. It is not deer meat."

Crinch's eartips grew red, then white, and he made a grave tactical error. He got mad.

"The whole damn bunch of you is lyin'!" he snarled. "I oughta lock all of you up!"

"You watch your tongue!" my grandmother said sharply, beginning to stiffen and straighten.

"Don't give me trouble, old lady!" Crinch shouted. "Or I'll lock you up with your worthless kid. If you got guts enough to call this worthless bum your kid."

That did it. Even though Uncle Al *was* kind of an old bum, you didn't go around telling my grandmother that. And you most certainly didn't accuse her of lying.

She expanded with awesome majesty, like a towering thunderstorm, and looked down on Crinch from miles in the sky. It was like one of those old calendar pictures of clouds with big grouchy faces in them which blew ice storms down on the hapless world. The air turned perceptibly warmer, sultry, and oppressive, as it does just before violent weather erupts.

The color faded from Crinch's crimson face, leaving him looking somewhat like last year's elm leaves. He knew he had gone too far.

"Mr. Crinch," she said with distaste, as if confronted by a dirty diaper. "You are a mean little man."

"You can't talk," Crinch blustered uneasily.

She strode forward, brushing him aside like a meddlesome puppy, and scooped up an enormous, wickedly-glinting butcher knife. Sunlight flashed from the keen blade and Crinch blanched, certain she was going to slit his sweetbreads.

But instead she turned and expertly shaved a steak from the moose meat. "You will come in the house and sit down," she said. It was not an invitation. It was a command. Unwillingly, he followed her into the kitchen, followed by the family.

"Sit down," she ordered. He sank gingerly into a chair, his expression that of a cornered rabbit. My grandmother turned to her stove and, with the expertise of 65 years of homemaking, had a skillet sizzling almost instantly.

She dropped the meat into the hissing hot frying pan. While it cooked, we all looked at my grandmother. She looked at Crinch and he looked resolutely at the floor.

She stabbed the steak out of the pan as if it were Crinch himself, plopped it on a plate, and set the food in front of the game warden along with a knife, fork, and salt shaker.

"Eat the meat," she said, folding her arms calmly.

"Well, I'm really not . . ."

"Mr. Crinch, you accuse me of lying and my son of venison poaching. I will not stand for that. Eat the meat."

"But I don't . . ."

"Mr. Crinch, if you don't eat enough of that meat to satisfy yourself that it is not venison, I am going to ask my sons to force it down your throat."

Uncle Floyd and the others growled and surged forward. Crinch cast a frightened look at them and hastily sawed off a chunk of rare moose and popped it into his mouth.

He chewed and chewed painfully, trying to reduce it to pieces small enough to slide down his dry, fright-constricted throat. We saw the whites of his eyeballs. The piece of moosemeat wouldn't go down.

"Well?" my grandmother demanded.

Crinch tried again to swallow, choked slightly, then tucked the meat in his cheek, like a chipmunk with an oversized nut.

"It ain't venison," he husked. "Can I go now?"

The BLUCCGWS picnic was the most talked-about social event since the dogs started fighting at Lucy Jorgenson's wedding and tore off her dress.

Scented invitations rose from the steaming grill and sent out irresistible tendrils, barbed olfactory hooks that snagged people out of the birch-clad hills who hadn't been to town since the bar gave free beer one New Year's Eve.

"Geez, Al!" moaned one bloated customer. "I'm about to split!"

"I think I'm gonna die," another sighed happily, refilling his plate. "But Heaven's gonna be a letdown after this."

Herbert Crinch, munching glumly on a chunk of roast, glared balefully at Uncle Al. "This ain't beef," he insisted doggedly. But he helped the vast assemblage swallow every scrap of the evidence.

Uncle Al volunteered to be chairman of the cleanup committee and he gathered up every bone in a tow sack and buried them all somewhere near the edge of the earth.

Uncle Floyd waited a month, then mounted the antlers over his back bar. Crinch saw them there and knew instantly what had happened.

He opened his mouth to say something and Uncle Floyd waited expectantly. But then Crinch thought of my grandmother, and he quietly closed his mouth.

THE SWEET SMELL OF VICTORY

Melody Hawkins was as delicious as her name, with a laugh that sparkled like wind chimes, shining hair flowing in a summer wind with the rich glow of molten gold.

Melody was a new-mown hayfield, a warm puppy, a trellis of blooming honeysuckle. I loved Melody Hawkins till the stars winked out and the universe became still.

Then there was Ace Swanson, a lout two years ahead of us in school. Ace Swanson, therefore, was an Older Man and doubtlessly irresistible to impressionable young girls——Melody Hawkins, if you have not guessed. He also drove his own car, while I still was in the bicycle age.

I thought maybe Melody liked me, for there were soft-eyed exchanges of confused glances over the rusty drinking fountain at decrepit old Birch Lake High School, a fleeting touch of fingers as I passed her the salt in the school cafeteria (her hand felt like a purring kitten), but I was afflicted with drymouth when it came to asking her for a date.

However, great events often erupt from diverse happenings that converge on a central point, like speeding, brakeless freight trains converging on a cringing roundhouse. One of those trains started chugging away the morning that I ran into Melody and her unattractive friend, Annabelle, in front of The Store, Birch Lake's inspirationally named drygoods business.

"Hey, hi, Melody!" I trilled, my voice tremulous from nerves.

"Hi, Bobby," she said, her voice a sweet lamb gamboling in a verdant field. "You sure have a nice tan."

Annabelle sneered at me.

"Hey, yeah. It comes from the sun," I babbled. "Listen!" in desperation, "how about going to the movie with me tomorrow night? I mean, it's John Wayne. Course, if you don't wanna . . ."

"Oh, that would be nice!" she said, rocking me with a stunning smile.

Annabelle sneered. Annabelle once hit me with half a brick when I called her a jerk. We were eight years old at the time and she never forgave me for not dying.

"Hey, Wartbrain!" The grating voice belonged to Ace Swanson, soul brother of Annabelle whose sparse vocabulary made him a veritable Hemingway of insult. He had overheard my invitation to Melody and he was not happy.

"You talkin' to me?" I quavered, wishing I dared to give him my Steve McQueen sneer, the one I had practiced in front of the mirror.

"Nah——I'm talkin' to the flies on the flypaper," he sneered (much like Richard Widmark) and Annabelle giggled and Melody bit off a quick smile and I considered oozing into the sidewalk cracks.

"Look," Ace said, throwing an arm around me that seemed to be built of a greasy T-shirt and the leaf spring off a back truck axle, "why don't you go home and play with your dollies while I take these chicks for a spin. How about it, chicks? Need a lift?"

"Sure!" Annabelle crowed quickly. "Come on, Melody!" She grabbed Melody's hand and dragged her into the stripped-down monstrosity Ace called a car. Ace quickly slammed the door and vaulted into the front seat, casting me a glance as if he were looking at dog mess.

Melody also looked at me and, in my despair, I thought Melody's expression was contempt.

Great knight in shining armor! Bitterly I turned toward the window of The Store and found I was looking at the doll display.

It was a mean night, but I resolved to stand firm on my date with Melody. Ace cornered me the next day as I was airing my bicycle tires at the Standard Station. He threw that arm around me again. It was like being embraced by a packing strap. "You got a date with Melody," he said flatly. It was not a question. "Take a health tip. Don't show up."

I couldn't think of a rejoinder that would leave me with my head. Ace punched me affectionately on the arm. It felt like a splitting maul. "Y'see, I kinda like ol' Melody. Ain't no point in her wastin' time on a squirt like you." He leered at me. He reminded me of a dogfish I once caught.

Ace no sooner had turned the corner than a soft voice which sounded like doves in a cedar tree said, "Bobby?" Were the angels calling me? "Bobby?" I looked up from my greasy bicycle. It was Melody. "I didn't mean to run off yesterday. But Ace kind of overpowers a person." She smiled wryly. "Guess I just don't know how to say no."

Oh, wonderful! I thought. Ol' Ace would be delighted to hear that. I made a grim resolution he must be stopped "at all costs" as they said in spy movies. I suspected the cost might be a couple of arms and a leg, all mine. "Listen," I said desperately, "I'll be by tonight about seven and we'll go to that show. Okay?"

"Okay," she said softly, and I felt about three times bigger than Ace Swanson. Until Melody left, taking pleasant unreality with her.

How to stop Ace? If only I could make him unacceptable, build some sort of wall around him, the big stinker.

The big stinker?

The big stinker!

Inspiration arced across my brain, an intuitive short circuit of Frankensteinian proportions. It was not the first time I'd been thus inspired and always I was blind to all possible trouble. There was the roadgrader incident and the time my cousin Hal and I wanted to exhibit the live bear cub at the annual street dance and the mother bear scattered a huge crowd and demolished a couple thousand dollars' worth of musical instruments and, well, those who knew me well instantly began to edge away when I announced an inspiration.

Especially my cousin Hal, frequent participant in my schemes. "I know how I'm gonna bomb ol' Ace right out of town," I said.

"Oh, geez!" Hal groaned, recognizing the symptoms of an inspiration.

"Skunk juice. Uncle Al's skunk juice."

Hal frowned, uncomprehending. But if I was involved and if Uncle Al was involved and if a skunk was involved, the potential for disaster was about 120 percent. The only person in the family who got into more trouble than I did was Uncle Al.

"He gets it from skunks he traps," I said. "He puts that stuff in a bottle. It's the real knock-you-on-your-can stink."

"What for?" Hal asked in awe.

I shrugged. "You never know when you're gonna have to skunk someone up."

Hal's eyes popped open. "You ain't gonna put that on Ace Swanson!" he breathed, drawing back from me as if I'd just announced I had infectious impetigo.

I smiled.

"He'll rip your arm off and beat you to death with it!"

"Trust me," I soothed.

"Sure," Hal sneered. "Let me know when I can go ice skating in Hell, too."

It was no trick to swipe the dusty bottle of skunk essence from the shed out back. The bottle seemed to emit a glow of confined power. It was like handling nitroglycerine and my palms were clammy. Ace Swanson wouldn't be fit to live with for six months, assuming he ever had been fit to live with.

"I got it all planned out," I told Hal. "Every night when Ace goes home he drives that rattlebomb of his under the big oak tree out on Double B Highway. A guy could lay out on the big branch that hangs over the highway and when ol' Ace rips by, why, just drop that canned woods puss right into the engine. He'll have it on the car and on him. Teach him to take the hood off his car."

Hal looked at me with something like respect, at least the closest he'd ever come to respect. The plan required timing and a bit of athletic ability, but it would work! By the time the drench of stink penetrated Ace's Neanderthal skull and he got the car stopped, I'd be about three miles away, picking up speed. He had enough enemies; he couldn't know for sure who did it and he certainly wouldn't be hanging around Melody Hawkins for quite awhile. He'd have to phone in his rough-hewn endearments long distance.

It was a beautiful evening for a bomb run. I stashed my bicycle carefully in the roadside brush. If Ace asked, I'd tell him I'd been on Mars when the skunk hit the fan. Fear tended to make me a fluent liar.

The broad, shelving limb of the old oak was comfortable. I stretched out on it with my cheek against the rough bark, clutching the bottle of stink and listening for the distant throb of Ace's hated hotrod.

And then it came, a distant mutter like thunder announcing an approaching storm. I glimpsed Ace's car, first a speck rounding the far bend, then a toy car, quickly growing larger. Ace's greasy hair flew in the turbulence and my lips drew back in a savage, snarling grin. Only seconds 'til I would have my revenge!

The car was upon me, its oversized rear wheels and heavy-duty shocks tilting it forward to present a perfect target. I cocked my arm. If I flipped the bottle as the radiator passed from my left eye's field of vision, the bottle should slant directly onto the hot engine, shatter, and the spray of horror would be blown by the fan all over good ol' Ace.

Then, a split second before I released the skunkbomb, an intense vision of what would come paralyzed me. Ace would see the bottle fall, would stand on his finely tuned brakes, would stop the car instantly, would disregard the terrible smell, would lumber back to the tree before I could get out of it, would pluck me off the limb like a rotten apple, and, amid eddying clouds of stench, would make head cheese of my tender adolescent flesh.

The vision was so terrifying that I lost my balance as the car swept beneath me, loosed a wild cry, and fell. Desperately I let go of the bottle and grabbed the limb with my fingertips. The bottle hit the pavement an instant before my feet did, long enough to shatter and spread concentrated horror in which I sprawled. I sat stunned as the sound of Ace's car faded and died.

It was so awful that it didn't even smell like skunk. It was a burning, choking cloud, like falling into the mouth of Hell. It surrounded me, ripped at my lungs. I don't remember much about the trip back to town. I stopped at every farm pond to scrub, but that was like baling the ocean with a fork.

And then I realized I had a date with Melody Hawkins in three hours. "What am I gonna do!" I whimpered. "What am I gonna do!" My problem no longer was Ace. Any whipping he could hand me would be a distinct pleasure compared to what I was going through.

I found Hal behind the ice house, contemplating an ant. "You ever eat an ant?" he called, spying me. "Remember when you ate that worm and Grandma thought you was nuts? I read somewhere ants is bitter."

There was a vagrant reversal of the prevailing breeze and Hal tumbled backward. "What the pie-eyed hell is that!" he cried. "You got a skunk!" He scrambled backward like a crab.

"You gotta help me. I got a date with Melody. What am I gonna do?" Hal didn't press me for details. He surmised my grand plan had come completely unglued. So his lack of faith was justified and he felt vindicated. He also felt vindictive.

"Wait 'til I get Uncle Al's gun. You can shoot yourself," he smirked.

"Very funny. What kills skunk stink?"

"A trip out of town for a year."

"Tomato juice!" I shouted. Hal's eyes got big, the way they did when he was convinced I'd really blown my cork.

"Huh?"

"You rub tomato juice on and it takes the stink out. Or maybe it's toothpaste? No, that's for fish stink. It's tomato juice."

"My God, Bobby, that stuff musta tore your brain or something."

"No lie!" I cried. "I read it in a women's magazine when I was looking at the underwear ads. You put on tomato juice and it kills the skunk stink."

Hal sighed.

"Grandma must have a billion tomatoes out in her garden," I said.

"She'd make you think skunk if she caught you messing with her tomatoes," Hal warned darkly.

"She's outa town," I said. "She won't miss a couple of tomatoes."

So it was that we crept into my grandmother's meticulous garden. I feasted my stink-bleared eyes on salvation in the form of juicy Rutgers, rugged Marglobes, hefty Beefmasters. I tiptoed down the weedless aisle between the ranked plants, for my grandmother made John Wayne by comparison look like a schoolyard sissy and one did not lightly trifle with her garden. Tentatively, I grasped a tomato and pulled it free. I took a deep breath and squashed it against my arm. The juice squirted and ran through my fingers and the acid smell penetrated slightly through the yellow fog that lay a thick, noxious nimbus over me.

Hal watched with the fascination of someone watching a cobra being milked. The devil invaded me and I hurled the pulped tomato .at him and splashed it off his shoulder.

"Hey, Creepo! I'll get you for that!" He charged forward, but thumped against the knobby wall of stink. Angrily he jerked a big, dark Rutgers off a handy vine and pegged it at me. I caught it, a nice one-handed grab, the way I took his double play flips when he played shortstop and I played second. I crushed it and rubbed the juice on my face.

Tomatoes began to fly back and forth. I wallowed in the growing pile of mashed tomatoes, rubbing the squishy pulp in my hair, my ears, my nose, my clothing. I slipped and slid in slimy tomato.

"WHAT IS GOING ON HERE!" The voice thundered over us like a cataclysmic avalanche. It was the Herculean snarl of an approaching tornado, a maelstrom of doom, the unearthly hoofbeats of the Four Horsemen, the ominous visage of the Angel of Retribution, the sound of mountains erupting, continents sinking, worlds colliding.

My grandmother had returned.

I loosed a wild cry and, streaming pulp and seeds, fled. An hour later, I crept into my bedroom and began to clean off the unpleasant dried film. As far as I could tell, I was largely defused. Sooner or later there would be a confrontation with my grandmother about my tomato patch antics, and sooner or later Ace Swanson would stuff a drive shaft up my nose. But tonight was mine and Melody's, a night of starshine and summer splendor.

She came to her door, dramatically backlighted by the hall light. The hall light made her honey hair shine. "Hi, Bobby!" The screen door creaked in the still night. Cicadas stridulated a summer song. The air was heavy with the muck of honeysuckle and newcut clover hay. There was a full moon, its chubby face astonished as always. Melody tucked her arm in mine. "I wasn't sure you'd want to go out with me after I went off with Ace," she said.

"Oh, leave that stupid car out of it and what does Ace have that I don't?" I asked, immediately regretting it, for had she wanted to she could have made a list, starting with muscles. However, the overriding question, as I quickly found out, was what I had that he didn't.

"Bobby, do you smell something funny?"

The game was up. "It's me," I said miserably. The romantic night was a mockery.

She looked incredulously at me. "You're kidding!"

Another dream up in smoke. Every time I tried to impress a girl, I wound up looking like one of the Three Stooges. It made me mad.

"If it hadn't been for that squarehead Ace Swanson, I wouldn't smell like a tomato-eatin' skunk!" I snarked. "You oughta go out with him. All he smells like is a crummy valve lifter!"

I jammed my hands in my pockets and wished I were wrestling wolverines on the tundra.

She frowned. "Ace? I don't care anything about him. He's a big dummy. But what's he got to do with, well, the way you smell?"

So I told her the whole sorry thing and at about the point where Hal and I started chunking tomatoes at each other, Melody Hawkins began to laugh. It really did sound like wind chimes.

"Bobby, you're so crazy I could kiss you!"

"You could! I mean, you can! I mean, if you want to."

"Can I hold my nose?" More wind chimes.

So she kissed me and I grinned foolishly and said, "Well, it'll probably wear off in a month or so," and figured I'd handle Grandma and Ace somehow.

Instead of going to the movie, we walked down to the lake and watched the moon ripple on the wind-ruffled surface and listened to a loon enjoying its manic sense of humor far out on the dark waters and I'd never been happier.

Melody sat upwind of me, but close enough that I caught her clean meadow scent. It certainly beat mine.

UNCLE AL'S DUCK SHACK

My Uncle Al's duck shack squatted tiredly at the edge of a marsh about two miles out of Birch Lake. It was on the high ground above the marsh where cattails nodded at rifts of bright-green duckweed and muskrats trundled busily about. Smartweed, rooted in the rich bottom muck, created food that attracted a small but reliable supply of ducks for Uncle Al and his hunting buddies.

The shack was an unpainted, splintery, rickety scrapbook of Birch Lake duck hunting history. Errant puffs of duck down drifted into the dark corners to join last summer's deceased spiders. Dust motes twinkled in the October sun, a sun that shouldered its way through grimy windows untouched by cleaning cloth at least since Uncle Al had won the lease in a sharpshooting match with a beered-up tourist from the Cities who had mistaken bleary eyes and a trembling hand as a sign of weakness. Little did he know that Uncle Al usually looked that way and still could shoot the eye out of a gray squirrel 60 yards away.

Faded, torn photographs of long-dead hunters were tacked randomly on the walls, dim memorials to once-vibrant hunters. A cracked wooden bluebill call hung forlornly from a bent nail. A rusty teakettle on the woodstove provided some humidity on a cold winter night. A pitted eight-gauge shotgun that must have weighed 20 pounds leaned tiredly against the fireplace, unused since the days of 25-duck bag limits. The maw of the fireplace was black from countless hot, popping fires. The floor creaked and sagged and there was old retriever hair on the two tattered throw rugs. The place smelled of coffee and tobacco and wet dogs.

There were several dozen duck decoys on the canted front porch, each with an anchor cord and weight wrapped securely about its painted neck, each staring patiently through the long off season with blank glass eyes.

It was a short walk down a well-worn trail through the cattails and reeds to the stout wooden blind. When alder leaves turned to gold and maples flamed, ducks began to filter into the marsh, announcing to each other and to passing cousins that this was a good place to rest before heading on south.

Uncle Al leased the marsh for a very small annual sum from the town bank, but there had been a problem for the past two years. The old banker had died and the new man had talked of selling the marsh. He would have sold it to Uncle Al, but Uncle Al never could have scraped up the cash. He had enough trouble making the lease payments. Mr. Pevely, the new banker, was a tight little man whose idea of a persuasive argument was hearing the sound of two coins rubbed together.

The shack held no charm for him. It and the swamp were unsightly and he did not believe a bank should hold properties that were unsightly. Not only was Uncle Al's duck shack an irritation, Uncle Al's appearance was, too.

"Mr. Pevely is running for church elder," my grandmother announced at supper one night in late autumn. "He thinks he's going to run the church the same way he runs that bank. He needs to learn a church isn't a business. He doesn't allow for the heart and the soul."

It was a long speech for my grandmother, who usually was content to issue terse no-argument commands. Still, her opposition was a guarantee that Mr. Pevely would not insinuate himself into the fiber of Birch Lake through the church. When she finished talking to the members of the flock, it was no contest. Mr. Pevely lost hand-ily and must have felt like a pup whose nose has been rubbed in a mistake.

Whatever Christian satisfaction she felt was short-lived, for the next day Uncle Al trudged in to dinner and slumped at the table, head buried in his hands. "They're gonna take my duck shack lease, Mama!" he cried in anguish, as close to tears as he'd been in nearly 60 years. "Pevely ain't gonna renew my lease!"

Pevely knew his legal structure would withstand any amount of moralistic heavy weather my grandmother could generate. "I'm sorry," he said with a tight little smile. "It's business."

"It's vindictiveness, that's what it is!" my grandmother stormed, completely helpless for once in her life.

"Call it what you like," Pevely said. "But on October 22nd, the lease reverts to the bank and I expect your son to have his junk cleaned out of my building."

That gave Uncle Al precisely one day of duck hunting. He chose me to go with him, perhaps because I was family, maybe because I represented the future. His own future was bleak. I think he liked to see the world through my eager young eyes.

We drove out to the shack in his rusty, rattly old pickup truck——not because it was too far to hike, but because riding was easier on old Sam, Uncle Al's aged Labrador retriever. Sam had come to Uncle Al in mid-life and had proven himself a sensational duck dog. Now he was arthritic and dim of hearing, but in his amber eyes there still shone the fire of a young dog, the spirit of the fine retriever he had once been.

The trees were turned and a bitter wind whistled across the marsh and sent me shivering deeper into my heavy coat as we stood on the sagging porch of the duck shack and watched the sun go down. "Weather front moving in," Uncle Al said. "Ought to bring in something. Maybe some bluebills or pintails. Maybe a few mallards."

I went to bed early and lay warm under a heavy quilted comforter, snuggled deep in the soft folds of an old feather mattress. Uncle Al sat at the tottery oilcloth-covered table, the flickering firelight casting gaunt patterns on his stubbly face. He held the old bluebill call between his gnarled hands and looked carefully around the shabby walls of the duck shack. He was saying goodbye.

The fire died during the night and early winter cold seeped quickly through the cracks and tatters of the old shack. Uncle Al got a fire going early in the rusty pot-bellied stove and I stood by it, swapping sides to equalize the searing heat on one side, the bitter cold on the other.

There had been a flight of ducks during the night. I knew it when we reached the shore of the marsh. The still, crisp, black night was filled with the chuckle and gabble of contented ducks. An occasional hen voiced hearty approval of this wonderful spot. There was no moon, no stars. Cloud cover lay low, promising low-flying birds. Sam brushed against me and I reached down and patted his rough, mist-dampened coat.

False dawn filtered through the marsh and the waxing light gradually showed us the decoys, bobbing slightly in a slight breeze. A flock of ducks whispered past, the rush of their wings loud in the still. Then it became light enough to shoot. Four teal flickered past so low and so quickly that neither of us could react. They splashed into the reeds just out of gun range, wagged their tails proudly and looked self-satisfied.

Uncle Al gestured. "Greenheads!" he whispered. We ducked our heads and he called in the circling birds with the skill of a lifetime. The ducks responded instantly, spilling air and side-slipping, their red feet splayed toward the decoy set.

We rose when the mallards were a dozen feet high and dropped two. Sam suddenly was in the water, though neither of us saw him leave the blind. He swam awkwardly, straitjacketed by the stiff fabric of his years. He collected the duck farthest out and brought it back. Uncle Al took the bird, a softness in his lined face. Sam splashed back into the chill water and retrieved the second duck with weary authority. When he brought it in, he was wheezing and obviously exhausted. But he sat at Uncle Al's feet, delivered the duck, then walked stiffly off a few feet before he shook the water from his gray-flecked coat. Uncle Al swallowed noisily.

"God, I hate to see that cheap chiseler get this place!" Uncle Al said to himself, or perhaps to Sam. The hunt was over. The magic that had been there evaporated and the day was only gray and cheerless. Without talking, we gathered the decoys, stashed them in the truck, along with the pitiful few belongings Uncle Al had at the shack.

The idea hit me that afternoon. I'd been thinking all day about Uncle Al and all the times we'd had together. The time we shot the moose together and the time he blew the block out of his pickup trying to shoot the buck deer and the time old Sam proved he was the world's greatest duck dog by retrieving a duck in a violent thunderstorm and nearly killing himself in the process——Uncle Al was worth thinking a lot about.

My inspirations occasionally were earthshaking, but not usually in a productive way. Even I had learned to be cautious when one of those blinding flashes came over me, like an intellectual fit. Still, what I had to lose was nothing compared to what Uncle Al had on the line. It was worth a try.

Friday was pay day at the mill and after the second shift quit at three, the bank always was full of big, whipcord-muscled lumberjacks and mill hands, cashing in their checks, getting ready to do their damndest to drink Birch Lake dry of Bruenig's lager before Sunday.

I ran upstairs to my bedroom, rummaged around in a drawer and found what I was looking for, stuffed it in my pocket and ran toward town and the bank. Sure enough, the building was filled with check-shirted Birch Lakers, stubble-faced men not too different than my Uncle Al, save they were steadily employed, fists like whang leather, suspended, boots oiled patiently by the light of coal oil lamps.

Mr. Pevely stood to one side watching the procession of loggers with a thin smile of satisfaction on his sharp face. Happiness to him was brisk cash flow. I stopped just inside the door, suddenly terrified at what I was thinking of doing. I shut my eyes, swaying with fright, and my mind's eye settled on the stiff old dog with the caring amber eyes. It was all I needed.

I took a deep breath and dragged out my bank book which showed a balance of $7.27. I shouted into the din: "I want my money! I want my money out of this bank!"

No one paid any attention to me, except one old lumberjack who frowned at me and said, "Hey, kid, you gotta stand in line like the rest of us."

The utter frustration of it, the combination of frustration and a smouldering rage that rapidly was turning into a full-fledged inferno, did what rage and frustration always, embarrassingly, did to me.

I began to cry. That made me even madder, if possible. I vaulted jerkily into the middle of the bank lobby, my movements stiff and uncoordinated because of my anger, leaped onto a spittoon, then to the middle of one of the tall tables provided for customers to fill out deposit slips. My foot hit a large brass ashtray and it shot down the marble tabletop, off onto the tile floor where it clanged like a gong. I couldn't have gotten more instant quiet if I'd shot off a cannon.

Every face turned toward me. I was beyond being scared now. I waved the bank book in the air and glared at Pevely.

"I want my money out of this crummy no-good bank!" I shouted at him as his mouth dropped open. "I got seven and a half in here and·I want it right now. You're takin' my Uncle Al's duck shack away from him outa being a damned mean old man and I ain't gonna give you nothing!"

I looked at the lumberjacks below me. "You all know my Uncle Al," I said. I looked down at a beefy, red-faced Norski whose mouth gawped in astonishment. "You know Uncle Al! He's the best guy in the world and that little piss ant is gonna take his duck shack away outa spite. It'll kill him if he loses it! Do what I'm doing—— take your money out of this bank! Put it over to Rice Lake if you gotta, but don't help old Pevely steal my Uncle Al's duck shack! It ain't right!"

Nobody moved.

Then Pevely, his face white, then red, shrieked, "Get out of my bank, you punk kid!"

He shoved a couple of men aside, hopping, he was so angry, reached for me. "Take your money out of here! He's a mean man!"

Pevely grabbed me by a pant leg and tried to drag me off the table. I pulled away. He reached with his other hand, caught the hole in the pants, worn through at the knee, and ripped the pant leg to my ankle.

There was a communal growl from the big men all around him, but Pevely was unaware of it. "Please!" I shouted desperately. "Help my Uncle Al out! You all know him!"

Pevely grabbed me at the knee, his hand slipped and his long fingernails raked scarlet grooves down the side of my leg.

That did it. A big hand caught Pevely by the scruff of the neck and he suddenly found himself suspended in midair. "Lay off that kid, Pevely," growled a basso-profundo with a Scandahoovian tinge.

"Put me down!" Pevely squeaked.

"What do you want from this guy?" rumbled the big lumber-jack.

"I want a forever lease for my Uncle Al on his duck shack," I said. "I want him to be able to hunt ducks there as long as he lives without having to worry about Pevely taking it away."

"How about it, Pevely?" the lumberjack asked, twisting Pevely around so his frightened eyes were close to the lumberjack's beefy face.

"You have no right——it's intimidation——I won't——you can't force," Pevely blustered.

"Pevely," the lumberjack said, his blue eyes narrowing to glinty little chips of ice. "There ain't a man in here don't like Al. You don't do what the kid here says, we'll jerk our money out of your jerkwater bank and if we pass the word around Birch Lake, won't be long 'til you don't have enough money to buy your morning cup of coffee. Al and the boy here, they're Birch Lake. You ain't." He set Pevely gently down.

Pevely looked around, appeared to suck a green persimmon. But business is business.

So there came to be tacked up alongside the dusty old bluebill call a framed lifetime lease which gave Uncle Al exclusive rights on the marsh and the duck shack.

We went out again the next day, Uncle Al and Sam and I. Mostly we just sat in the blind and watched the ducks fly against the wind that bent the reeds and made them whisper to each other.

When I started for home that evening, I looked back at the duck shack. Uncle Al and Sam stood in the doorway, warmed by the lowering sunlight, two old guys who had been together in their old duck shack too long to be separated from it.

I swallowed hard and waved goodbye.